NIGHTWATCH

NIGHTWATCH
A NOVEL

JOHN LEAX

Zondervan Books
Zondervan Publishing House
Grand Rapids, Michigan

Nightwatch
Copyright © 1989 by John Leax

Zondervan Books
are published by Zondervan Publishing House
1415 Lake Drive, S.E.
Grand Rapids, MI 49506

Library of Congress Cataloging-in-Publication Data

Leax, John.
    Nightwatch : a novel / by John Leax.
      p.   cm.
    ISBN 0-310-21860-8
1. Title.
    PS3562.E262N54   1988   89-31522
    813′.54—dc20   CIP

All rights reserved. No part of this publication may be reproduced by any means, except for brief quotations in printed reviews, without the prior permission of the publisher.

Printed in the United States of America

89 90 91 92 93 94 / DH / 10 9 8 7 6 5 4 3 2 1

For Ron

*For now we see through a glass, darkly;
but then face to face:
now I know in part;
but then shall I know
even as also I am known.*

Part One
1950

1

The Cabin

Mark carried the toy rifle across the front of his body the way he'd seen his uncle carry a shotgun pheasant hunting. Unconsciously he watched the light play along the blue of the barrel as he moved it ahead of him, and he delighted in the comfortable feel of the plastic, woodgrained stock in his hands. As he went through the field of blossoming Queen Anne's lace and goldenrod, heading for the woods behind his house, he felt the sun warm his back through his tee shirt, the grass roughly brush his thin forearms and elbows, and the occasional wetness from spittlebugs.

His birthday present, the toy rifle, had been the object of a running argument between his mother and father. It had started when Mark, envious of his older cousins, had asked for a BB gun, a Red Ryder Special. Mark's wish seemed reasonable to his father, a gentle man who had given up hunting when he'd married. He remembered the pleasure he'd enjoyed as a boy loose with a .22. But Mark's mother would have no part of it.

"Tom Baker," she'd said, "I won't have the boy shooting songbirds."

"I think Mark won't do that," he'd answered.

"Then it's settled," she'd snapped. "You know boys can't be happy plinking cans."

"Nancy," he'd tried, "other kids have them. I could forbid him to shoot living things."

"That'll only make him disobey," she'd answered.

On that he knew she was right, and he'd given in, but when he found the toy replica in the hardware store, he bought it without consulting her. Though she'd been annoyed, she admitted it was no different than the cap guns she allowed, and finally accepted it as a compromise.

Mark loved it. That it shot only a puff of air did not matter to him. It looked real, and when he fired it, it kicked against his shoulder and cracked like a .22.

When Mark stepped from the field into the woods, the sudden coolness and darkening light stopped him like a vague fear. He stood staring down the path. It was familiar to him. He went down it nearly every day, but never without stopping to look furtively about, breathing deep, tucking his head slightly, and tugging at his pants, as if hitching up his courage. The path angled down a steep bank and curved across a small wooden bridge spanning a trickle of a creek that ran dry in late summer. The first red maple leaves of the fall, rustling like water, curled and blew in the stream bed. Mark's uncles and his father had cleared the path, cutting locusts from the bank and using them as poles for the bridge two summers before, the same summer they'd built the cabin for him.

That summer had been a hard one for Mark. It seemed to him his cousins owned the woods. He could hear them tearing about on hot afternoons, but his mother had ruled him too small to join them. He knew what they were doing. They had come to the yard and told him. Armed with hatchets and camp axes, they were hacking, chopping at trees and bushes, breaking branches and dragging them to a high spot in the old orchard where they built a fort. Some days they divided into teams, one occupying the fort, the other attacking up the hill, hurling green apples like grenades. Those days Mark would stand at the edge of the woods and imagine himself one of the attackers. He'd charge up the hill, dodging and ducking, until at the wall of the fort, he'd leap high and pound the defenders with missiles.

One afternoon late in July, when the sound of the apple wars reached him, Mark had slipped into the shadow and down the bank. He climbed over deadfalls, brushed spiderwebs from his face, and made for the sound. He was wearing his Davy Crockett cap, and at first he felt like the mountainman from Tennessee; but it was further to the orchard than he thought, and by the time he reached it he was scratched and sweaty.

"Friend or foe?" a voice demanded from the fort.

"Friend!" he answered.

"Foe!" it yelled back. An apple whizzed past his head, smacking into a tree trunk and spattering.

"Friend!" Mark cried. Another apple answered. He ducked, but apples were everywhere. He turned to run. An apple, hard as a rock, caught him in the ear. The whole side of his head burst into pain, he tripped, and pitched to the ground in tears.

Voices surrounded him. When he looked up, his cousins stood over him. "You okay?" one of them asked. "We didn't mean to hitja. We was jist playin."

Mark sniffed and wiped his nose on his shoulder.

Chucky, the oldest of the cousins, took charge. "Come on guys," he said, "let's take him up to the fort."

Delighted, Mark rubbed the tears away and tried to ignore the stinging warmth of his ear. At the fort, Chucky asked, "You want to join the gang?"

Instantly, the cousins protested, "He can't join the gang!" But Chucky cut them off.

"Of course he can. He jist hasta be initiated."

The protests ceased, and the cousins grinned.

"You want to be initiated?" Chucky asked.

Slowly, without understanding, Mark nodded his head.

"Good. You gotta trust me. Okay?"

Again Mark nodded.

"Hold your hands out."

Mark raised his hands. Chucky undid Mark's belt, pulled it from his waist, and wrapped his wrists tightly. Unable to use his hands, Mark bit his lip.

"Now turn around so you can't see me," Chucky ordered.

"Why?" Mark asked.

"You want to be initiated or don't you?"

"Yes."

"Then turn around."

Mark obeyed. Then he wished he hadn't, for Chucky grabbed his pants and jerked them down. A roar of approving laughter erupted from the cousins. When Mark bent to reach his pants, Chucky pushed him, and he fell in a tangle. "All the way off guys," Chucky yelled. The cousins pounced. Mark fought, but they held him down, one of them sitting on his head to halt his fury.

"The little sucker's bit my bum."

"Get his underpants too."

Mark thrashed and heaved but in the end, they stripped him and ran off leaving him to find his way home in only his tee shirt and coonskin cap.

The next day Mark's father and uncles cut the locusts and cleared the spot for the cabin.

Sunlight, breaking through the locust canopy, dappled the path. Mark's moment of apprehension passed, and he trotted down the path, across the bridge, and up the small ridge towards his cabin, the rifle hanging from one hand. Small, eight feet square, the windowless cabin had a shed roof six feet high at the peak. It was made of plywood and was stained dark brown. The doorway, which had no door, was cut into a front corner and faced down the path. Cooler than the woods and dark, except for the splash of light in front of the door where he sometimes lay to read, the cabin was Mark's base of operations. By adult decree none of his cousins were allowed even to visit.

Inside, Mark leaned his rifle in the corner nearest the door and crossed directly to the opposite corner where he had a nail keg chair with a lift-out seat. Under it Mark kept the treasures that gave rise to his explorations. He removed the seat and laid a fossil shell, a crayfish carapace, two blue jay feathers, a milkweed fish still in the pod, and a piece of rotting belt in the light. He put the seat back and settled down to think about where he had found each item and whether he should return to search for another. In itself the crayfish carapace was the most interesting object in his collection, but the rotting belt was the newest, and its story was at once frightening and fascinating.

2

A Fragment of Belt

Several days before, on his way home from school, Mark had been descending the narrow reddog lane through the thickest woods with Sammy Taylor and Dickie Rich. Though Sammy and Dickie were both two years older than Mark, they were all in fourth grade. Mark knew that both made bad grades and that the teachers considered them rough and poor friends, but he liked being with them, and they got along. Neither ever teased him, in fact they protected him. Once Dickie had bloodied Chucky's nose when he started to tell a group of girls about stealing Mark's pants. And Sammy had invited him into the old farmhouse where he lived with his grandparents.

* * *

The house had been dark, and it smelled close and musty the way old houses containing old lives always smell. Sammy had had him wait alone in the entry while he went into the kitchen. As he stood looking curiously first up the foot-worn wooden stairs and then into the parlor with its drawn drapes and covered furniture, Mark imagined himself in a house from a grotesque fairy tale. And then Sammy's grandmother, stooped, but round and laughing, stepped into the hall.

"Come in. Come in," she said. Her voice, though scratchy and broken as if it weren't used often enough to be dependable, sounded welcoming and trustworthy. Mark had followed her immediately. The kitchen, however, overwhelmed him. A wave of heat from a huge black coal stove seemed to push him back. His face flushed and he stopped.

"Too hot for young folks," Sammy's grandmother chuckled. "Old bones. Old bones need to keep warm." She motioned across the room to where Sammy's grandfather sat at the kitchen table sorting pennies he had dumped from quart canning jars. "Take the window chair. Cold comes off the glass."

Mark had done what he was told and sat watching the old man. Dressed in a frayed wool shirt and dirty gabardine slacks, he silently studied the pennies through a magnifier. Sammy crossed the kitchen with two glasses of milk and spoke loudly in his ear. "This is Mark."

The old man grunted.

"Find anything good?" Sammy asked.

His grandfather looked up. Several days' growth of white whiskers rimmed his face. He pursed his lips, loosening them to speak, and roared, "No! Nothin but doubles! Never find anything anymore!"

Sammy laughed, "That's cause you got everything."

"Yep," the old man said. "Got prid near every penny there is to get." He turned to Mark. "You save pennies?"

"No sir," Mark answered.

"What? Say what?"

"No sir," Mark said, almost shouting.

"Then comere, I'll show you."

When Mark stood close to see, he smelled urine and garlic, but he held himself steady, breathed through his mouth, and listened as the old man explained mint marks and told him some pennies were worth 50 cents or more. Finally Mark said, "I've got to go now. I didn't tell my mom I was stopping anywhere."

The old man gave him two Indian Heads to start a collection and made him promise to visit again. "Sammy doesn't bring many friends in," he bellowed as Mark went out the door.

* * *

The three were halfway down the lane when Dickie stopped. "Either you guys wanna smoke?" he asked.

Both shook their heads. "Too close to home," Sammy explained.

"Well, I'm gonna have one." Dickie jumped the ditch at the edge of the lane, knelt on the bank, and rooted about in the bushes until he found a cookie tin. "I keep my stash here so old Miss Primface won't catch them on me at school." He sat back on the bank, reclining like a laborer after a long morning's work, and lit up.

"You gotta try this, Mark. My old man says there's

nothin like it to relax the mind and make the troubles go away."

Mark squirmed. "Not today," he said, "too close to home."

Dickie blew a slow cloud of smoke at the sky. "You guys know a man hanged himself in these woods?" he asked.

"When?" Sammy challenged.

"Before you was born."

"Then howdchu know?"

"My brother told me. Says this guy used his belt to hang himself from a big old tree cause his wife ran off."

Mark turned and looked over his shoulder into the woods. Thick scrub grown over with vines made an impenetrable wall behind him. He could see nothing through it, but he imagined the dark, loamy smell of the earth under the trees, and he felt the same uneasiness, the rolling, wavelike feeling that both attracted and repelled him that he got when Dickie talked about what his brother did with girls.

"You show me the place," Sammy had demanded.

"Sure," Dickie answered. "We gotta go through the cattail swamp."

They had gone down the lane, crawled through the barbed wire fence into the abandoned cow pasture, and walked along the creek at the edge of the woods until they reached the swamp. They went the long way through a thick growth of saplings and small oaks and out into a damp, shadowed, open space under a wolf tree, the gnarled old oak four feet in diameter that had seeded the hillside. No light reached the earth under the tree. The air hung heavy and still. Mark felt he had come to a place where mysteries lived, and he hadn't known whether he was excited or afraid, or if fear and excitement were the same thing.

They stood staring at the tree. Then Dickie, breaking the spell, strolled up to it. "Try to put your arms around this mother," he said. When neither Mark nor Sammy moved he ordered, "Come on. See if we can reach around it."

Mark recoiled when Dickie's hand touched his. The clammy flesh was strange, soft and yielding, a frightening contrast to the rough bark he pressed his body and face against. Stretching to reach Sammy, he let his fingers slip from Dickie's. He could touch one, but not the other. The tree was too big for them.

Then Sammy shouted, startling both of them, "Look up."

From one of the lower branches reaching horizontally over their heads, a fragment of belt dangled.

"Geez!" Dickie whispered. "I thought my brother was bulling me."

Mark had watched Dickie climb onto Sammy's shoulders and rip the belt down, and when Dickie had broken it into pieces and offered him one, saying, "This is the deadman's booty," he had taken it without speaking. He had felt himself growing weak and tired, as if he were awake far past his bedtime listening to adult conversation in the room below, and he had leaned motionless against the tree until Sammy and Dickie were far down the hill, and he had to run to catch them.

When they were back in the sunlight, they giggled and strutted, "I woulda liked to seen him, wouldn't a you?" Sammy asked.

"Bet his face woulda been all black," Dickie answered.

Mark had said nothing. Shyly he had touched the piece of belt in his pocket; it had been damp, and it had felt alive.

3

Wolf Tree

Mark got up from his chair, crossed the cabin and picked up the piece of belt. He'd asked his father if anyone had ever hanged himself in the woods.

"No," his father had said. "Why?"

"Dickie told me someone did."

"Don't be listening to him. He tells tales."

Relieved, Mark thought for a moment he might ask what it was Dickie's brother did in the woods with girls, but when he'd asked once before, his father had ignored him, so he went to his room and read.

In his hand the belt felt old and rotten, robbed of mystery and appeal by his father's denial of Dickie's story. He stuffed it in his pocket, replaced everything else in the seat, picked up his rifle, and stepped out of the cabin. Behind it, he slid down the bank into the gully of another small creek and headed downstream. He went slowly, stopping often to look for salamanders under stones and to blast imaginary bobcats and panthers in the trees. When he saw a pileated woodpecker, he whipped up the rifle to fire, but catching the living bird in his sights, did not pull the trigger. The woodpecker, oblivious to his presence, banged at a tree making a hard drumming sound that carried through the woods. Mark liked the flash of red as the head beat back and forth and the strips of wood that flew from the tree. Accidentally he made a noise that frightened the bird, sending it in a clatter of wings to a distant tree. He lowered the rifle, approached the tree, and examined the chunks of wood torn from the trunk. He gathered several to take back to his chair and stuffed them into his pocket with the belt before going on.

The stream grew wider as it descended, meandered into the open, and spread into the cattail swamp. Mark walked along its edge. Frogs plunged in little bursts of mud ahead of him. He'd tried to catch them often enough to know they were too quick for him, so he didn't try again, but just at the edge of the water, near a spot from which one had jumped, he saw a small hole about an inch across rimmed with mud. Sammy had told him large, blue-shelled crayfish lived in such holes. Determined to find out if Sammy told the truth, Mark knelt in the mud.

He stretched over the water and drew his hand towards the hole thinking to hook his fingers in it and dig it up. Then he remembered the pincers on the carapace in his cabin. The blue crayfish, if Sammy wasn't lying, had pincers big enough to squeeze blood from a finger. He wiped his hand on his pants and thought. He picked up a thin stick and slid it into the hole. Surprised, he felt something take hold of it and pull. Slowly, being careful not to rip it from the grasp of whatever had grabbed on, he withdrew the stick. A pair of pincers two inches long, one of them gripping the stick, emerged. They were followed by a hard, insect-like head. Tentatively Mark reached for the body. It shot backwards into the hole.

He found a larger stick, crawled back on the grass to a spot from which he could see the hole without being seen, guessed the direction it ran, pushed the stick partway into the ground, and waited. He was still and patient. Ten minutes later, the crayfish reemerged. Mark leaned on the stick, driving it deep into the mud through the crayfish tunnel. Its retreat blocked, the crayfish pivoted on its tail to scuttle backwards through the water, but Mark caught it neatly by its back and lifted it without being pinched.

The live crayfish was unlike the bleached carapace in the cabin. About five inches long, iridescent blue, it curled and uncurled its muscular lobster tail and waved its pincers, grasping angrily at the air. Mark held it so he could look into its face. Then he gave a finger to one of the pincers. The claw clasped his skin. It hurt, but it didn't, as Sammy had said it would, draw blood. And expecting it, he didn't even wince.

He opened his hand palm up and placed the crayfish on his fingers. It spun to face him, raising its pincers to do battle. But its movement tickled, and he flinched. The crayfish flipped to the ground. Mark caught it again and set it back in the water. Released, leaving a swirl of mud, it darted backward into deep water almost as quickly as a frog.

Mark pulled the stick from the hole, stood up, and

saw mud down the front of his legs. He brushed at it, gave up, crossed the swamp, jumping from grass clump to grass clump, muddying his shoes as well, and started up the scrub-covered slope towards the wolf tree. From the full sunlight of the swamp, through the broken shade of the saplings, he moved towards the near dark under the oak. The air, cool and pleasant on his skin, settled like dust on his imagination. Though he believed his father's word, under the influence of the shadows and the memory of Sammy's sudden shout, it had no power. He approached the tree fearing terrible things could happen at its base.

Sunlight had pierced the canopy, illuminating the tree and turning the air golden under its branches. It looked to Mark as if it were filled with glory. He wanted to climb it, rest in the highest crotch he could reach, and look out into the valley without being seen. But the lowest branch was beyond him. He stood gazing as the wind worked the leaves into a light-filled shimmer. When it dipped to tousle his hair, he felt he could raise his arms and be borne upward into the air.

But the wind did not lift him. Bearing voices, it woke him from his reverie.

"We safe here?"

"Couldn't be safer."

"You sure Dickie ain't sneaking around."

"I spooked him. Told him a guy hanged himself from this tree."

"Devil."

"You bet."

The words fell like leaves. Mark stood silently, rocking the rifle on the pivot of his finger in the trigger guard. Then he backed softly into the scrub and worked his way around the tree to where he could see what

Dickie's brother did in the woods with girls. His eyes fixed, he dug in his pocket past the woodpecker chips to the belt. He pulled it out and let it drop. Deliberately, he raised the rifle and took aim at the couple on the ground. In his sight they rose and fell. A sourness, like the sourness of sickness burned his throat. Tears blurred his vision. They swam before him, and he pulled the trigger.

At the sharp crack, the girl shrieked. Dickie's brother swore loudly, jumped to his feet, clutched his pants, and grabbing the girl's arm dragged her behind the tree.

Mark fled down the hill, through the swamp, and part way up the creek bed towards the safety of his cabin before stopping to see if he had been followed. When he was sure he hadn't, he sat down and discovered he was sobbing. Angry, he rubbed his eyes with a hard twisting of the heels of his palms.

"Damn dirty liars," he said to himself savoring the harsh alliteration of the forbidden words. A rage, stronger than anything he'd ever felt, swelled in him. He stood and screamed at the sky, "God damn dirty liars!" The words tasted like blood. He spit them at the ground. Then he fired his rifle. He fired it, from his hip, again and again, jerking the lever away from the stock, slamming it back, and pulling the trigger.

Bam!
Bam!
Bam!

Out of control, he worked the lever once more catching the fingers of his left hand as he slammed it back. Howling, holding the rifle by the barrel, he whirled and smashed it against a tree.

"Oh no!" he cried. "Oh no, no, no!"

The sun broke through the leaves shifting in the wind and played dancing spots before his eyes. They circled and spun, a dizzying swirl of light. He leaned against the tree and covered his eyes. The sun died, and the woods settled. His hand throbbing, he picked up his rifle, studied the splintered stock, and trudged up the gully.

Coming from the woods, Mark saw his father across the backyard. He paused, looked at the broken rifle in his hand and considered taking it back to the cabin or trying to hide it against his leg and sneak by unnoticed, but he didn't care. He walked directly to him and wordlessly handed him the shattered toy. His father took it and turned it over in his hands. He looked from it to Mark, noting the muddy knees and wet cuffs of his pants and the tear-streaked dirt on his face.

"Have a bad time?" he asked.

"I fell," Mark said. "I was running down a hill and wasn't looking and fell. The rifle hit against a tree when I rolled over."

"I see," his father said. Without thinking, he tried to straighten the stock. It snapped in his hands. "Well," he said, "looks like this will be a trick to fix."

Mark stared blankly.

"You do want me to fix it?" he questioned.

Mark didn't care. The rifle was a broken toy he was done with, but he heard in his father's voice what seemed to be some unspeakable need, and he answered, "If you can."

His father smiled. "Come watch."

In the basement Mark watched as his father traced the broken stock onto a piece of pine, cut it out, placed it in a vise, and then shaped it with a draw knife. Mark wanted to be happy, but the curls of white wood, falling to the floor, turned in his sight to pale flashes of thigh in shade and sunlight. He looked at his father. He was serene, humming to himself, forgetting everything but the wood, as he worked. Slowly Mark slipped the woodpecker chips from his pocket and dropped them into the shavings under the workbench.

"Do you think I'll be big enough for a real gun next year?" he asked.

"We'll see," his father answered.

Part Two
1956

1

Escape

Mrs. Baker, her hands in dishwater, looked out into the yard where Tom was already involved in his Saturday morning routine of lawn care and gardening. Behind her, Mark hunched, his elbows on the table, in the breakfast nook downing his second bowl of cornflakes. Though her talk seemed casual, Mark was on guard.

"It just seems strange. Every other scout trip you've gone on has left Friday night."

"Yeah. This came up kinda sudden."

"How's that?"

"Well, you know, the honor court is coming up, and a coupla guys need to get a trip in for badges, and we kinda talked Mr. Delaney into going up to Lemon Hole. Only a few of us are going."

"I didn't think you were working on anything."

"I'm not. I just happened to be there."

"You ought to, you know."

"Ought to what?"

"Work on something. You could be an Eagle if you wanted."

"Aw Mom, you know I've got other things now."

"But you're going on this trip. It wouldn't take much. I think you've been hanging around that Dickie, and you're ashamed of being a scout."

Mark raised his bowl to his mouth and drank the leftover milk.

"Mark!"

"Sorry. You weren't supposed to see that." He got up and crossed the room to dump the bowl in the dishwater. "It's okay Mom," he said, putting his arm around her and giving her a quick kiss. "I'm a good boy."

He turned to go, but she stopped him, "Not so fast, young man."

"What now?"

She washed a glass and rinsed it carefully, taking too long. Mark looked at the clock. "You've got time," she said. "I was just thinking. Tomorrow's communion. Mr. Delaney wouldn't schedule a trip on communion Sunday. He's an elder."

"I told you, he didn't schedule this. It just came up. He probably agreed without thinking and is going so as not to break his word."

"But what about you? Don't you think you should be there?"

"Yeah, probably. But you know. I said I'd go, and I can't back out now."

"No, I guess not. Sometimes though, I wish you were more interested." She sighed. "Oh well, time spent with Mr. Delaney is time well spent. Have a good time."

2

Water Snake

When he left the house, Mark cut cross country through the woods past his crumbling cabin, crossed the creek, and picked up one of the old mining roads that led out to the strip mines. The walking was more difficult than he expected. Low hanging branches and twining grapevines turned the trail into a tunnel and caught at the battered army rucksack he'd stuffed with gear, threatening to tear it from his back, and he was glad to step into the light at the edge of the mines. But there a tangle of blackberry canes blocked his way and scratched his legs through his jeans as he pushed forward. Once he was in the open, the sun beat down on his neck, and reflecting from the shiny gray stones, beat up at his face as he labored along between the cut and the waste pile of the desolate mine. On its banks scraggly sumacs, tall, bearded purple and red, grew above the thistles and burdocks. Chickadees and goldfinches set them bouncing as they flitted from branch to branch like notes on the wavering staffs of light that rose from the hot stones and floated before his eyes.

Near the end of the mine where the path forked, Mark stopped. One branch veered right and climbed to the top of the cut. The other descended steeply into the gorge, a dead end that collected and held a pool of water. Mark was hardly a mile from home, but he was sweat-soaked and tired. His rucksack, its iron frame designed to shape a load across the back of a man, rubbed uncomfortably against his narrow shoulders and dug into his thin hips. It felt as if it weighed more than he did, and the rope sling he'd rigged to carry his sleeping bag chafed, raising a welt on his neck. He imagined the water closing over him as his body sliced through its still, warm surface into the cool center of its depths. He shucked off his pack and ran down the path unbuttoning his shirt as he went.

Cattails grew in the mud along the near edge of the pool. A small ledge ran past them to the deep water. Mark stripped, dropping his clothes in a pile, and started along it. The sun was hot on his nakedness, but a slight touch of shifting air he had not been able to feel under the weight of his pack cooled him, sending ripples of anticipation over his flesh. The small stones of the ledge ground under his feet, and he stepped carefully, rolling his sole slowly from heel to toe to take the sharp edges without pain. He was halfway from the cattails to the deep water when he suddenly recoiled, jumped backwards, stomped hard on a rock, lurched awkwardly over the shallows, and then caught his balance. A water snake, three feet long and thick as his wrist, slid a scraping, lazy slither into the water. Mark stooped and grabbed a large flat stone. The snake, swimming easily, its head out of the water, its thick body hanging below it undulating, propelling it forward, moved steadily away. Mark watched until it reached the middle of the pool. Then he threw the rock. His hand and his eye were one. The stone skipped at the snake's head.

For an instant, as if struck dumb, suspended in a confusion of fear and joy, Mark was still. When he moved, he whispered, "Gees. Ain't nobody gonna believe this." A cold hollowness, a cave in his heart, opened within him, and he watched the snake roll slowly, white belly up, then sink, a broken, wavering rope to the bottom. Slow circles from the skipping stone broke on each other and washed to the shore at his feet. He stared until the water was still, then turned away. He could not follow the snake's descent into the cool.

As he dressed, the dull roar of trailer trucks rumbling along the highway on the other side of the ridge hurried him. He swung the rucksack onto his back, shrugged his shoulders to settle it, picked up his sleeping bag, and ducked his head through the sling. The weight of the pack hung lopsided, causing him to lean into the irritation of the rope. He tucked his thumb between it and his neck, held it off the welt, and set a quick pace up the path. But he did not keep it up. He slowed and fell into a plodding trudge, discomfort buzzing about him, biting like a host of deerflies.

At the crest of the hill, he paused and looked back into the gorge. He stood, burdened like a pilgrim, and scrutinized the water for the impossible, telling wedge of resurrection swimming for the shore. The pool, placid in the sunlight, blandly reflected the yellow-gray clay banks. He turned towards the highway. A wide, bramble-free hayfield sloping away from him rose and fell like a silent surf in the wind. Across it, beside the highway he could see a small copse of aspens and in their shade, balanced casually on the guardrail, a waiting figure. Drawing a final hot breath, he waded into the ocean of grass and started down.

3

Bullrope

"It took ya long enough to cross that field," Dickie said.

"It's a hot day," Mark answered, dropping his sleeping bag beside Dickie's pile of gear and twisting out of the rucksack. "Been here long?"

"Coupla smokes. Want one?"

Mark took the pack of Luckies, tapped a cigarette loose, and lit up. "Any trouble getting away?"

"Naw. My old lady doesn't care what I do."

"Mine does."

"Give you a hard time?"

"Checked me out pretty good. I told her I was going with the scouts, and she almost got onto me. I thought she was going to call Delaney, but then she dropped it."

"What'll you tell her tomorrow?"

Mark stepped over the guardrail and faced back up the field. "I'll think of something." He rounded his shoulders against the ache from the pack, sat down stretching his feet in front of him, and reclined against a guardpost. Sunlight dappled his face through the aspen. "I killed a snake on the way over," he said.

"Yeah?"

"A big water snake at the mine pool. I let it swim away, then nailed it with a stone from thirty feet. Really stupid." He drew on his Lucky, held the smoke in his mouth, and exhaled. A quick twist of smoke rose before him. He fell silent and closed his eyes, giving it time to thin and curl away in the air. When he opened them, he was looking up into the aspens. The pale leaves caught every shimmer of breeze. In the bright sunlight the highest branches seemed to be transfigured, as if they were coated with ice or glowing from burning heartwood. He stared, half focused, afraid to blink. His mind saw more than his eyes, sought words to hold it before him but failed. He let it go and shut his eyes. The quaking of the earth beneath the weight of the speeding trucks trembled in his thighs and rose through his body. He gave himself to the shaking and waited, expecting some revelation, but the drone subsided in the darkness. A coolness passed over his body. He looked up.

A cloud obscured the sun.

The branches were merely branches.

His vision had been a trick of light.

Mark sat forward. "You get the rope I told you to?"

"No sweat."

"Lemme see it."

"Yes Sir!" Dickie mocked. He slipped off the

guardrail and heaved his pack aside with his foot, revealing two coils of inch-thick bullrope. "I swiped it from the old man's service truck when he stopped home for coffee."

"He know?"

"I said I swiped it. He might know it's gone, but he don't know where it's gone."

Mark traced a square in the dust beside him, crossed it from corner to corner, and snubbed his Lucky out in the center. From the corner of his eye he watched Dickie watch him. He imagined shouldering his pack, crossing the field, and returning home. His mother, surprised, would ask questions, but he could answer them. He could say Mr. Delaney remembered communion and called it off. She'd give him a strange look and then buy it. He knew she would. She always bought his stories because she wanted them to be true.

"Something bothering you?" Dickie asked.

Mark shrugged. "I guess not. Not if it doesn't bother you."

"Nothing bothers me, Scout," Dickie laughed.

Mark grinned. "Then let's move."

Dickie stepped to the roadside and without lifting his arm, as if that would indicate too much desire, raised a thumb to the passing cars. After several had sped by, he began saluting as they vanished.

"Knock it off," Mark said. "No one will give us a ride with you flippin birds."

A farm truck slowed, pulled off the road, and stopped about fifty yards past them.

Mark grabbed up his pack and sleeping bag and started to run.

"Hold on!" Dickie snapped. "He's backing up. Help me with this rope."

3

How Far?

Twenty minutes later, the truck jolted to a halt at a dirt turnoff. As Mark and Dickie hauled their gear from the bed, the farmer leaned out his window and spit a dark streak of tobacco juice, cratering the dust at their feet. "You boys sure someone knows where you're going? It ain't safe going in that cave alone."

"There's two of us," Dickie said.

"Man got stuck in there years ago. Died a the cold."

"I know the spot," Mark said. "It's been dug out."

Dickie rested his pack on the side of the pickup and slipped his arms through the straps. "Our folks know when to expect us back," he said. He bent and picked up the coils of rope, looped them over his shoulder, straightened awkwardly, and spoke, moving off, "It's a ways up that hill."

Mark glanced up at the farmer. "Guess I better get along too. Thanks for the ride."

"Watch out for snakes," the farmer warned. "Rattlesnakes and copperheads both like caves. And they don't always rattle."

"Well, if we can't be good, we'll be careful," Mark answered.

The farmer, gave him a hard look, spat, jammed the truck into gear, and lurched onto the road. As he pulled away, he said something more, but the roar of his engine covered it. Mark figured it was just as well and turned away.

Dickie was thirty yards up the road. Annoyed, Mark thought for a moment to catch up, but he knew Dickie. To try too obviously to catch him would start a race, and Mark knew by the weight of his pack he wanted to walk easy. He set a pace that would slowly close the gap between them and followed.

The road, shaded by two rows of maples, ran straight from the highway for several hundred yards until it reached an old cellar hole and a collapsed barn. There, instead of climbing out of the valley, it curved, always away from the sounds of traffic, into the aspen woods along the base of the hill. About a mile on, where the road dipped to ford a wide, shallow stream, Mark caught Dickie.

"Wait up," he said. "We don't cross the stream."

"Where to then?" Dickie asked.

"Up there." Mark pointed to a narrow path that looked as if it had been made by fishermen along the stream.

"How far?"

"Two miles to the campsite. Another mile to the cave."

"Why don't we camp at the cave?"

"No water."

Dickie dumped his pack off. "You wanna smoke?"

"Naw," Mark said. He wanted to sit down while Dickie smoked, but he was still smarting at Dickie's head start, and he wanted to pay him back. "Let's keep going." He stepped onto the path before Dickie could get into his pack, and knowing there was no place wide enough for Dickie to pass him, set a slow, deliberate pace. Mark was sure his packframe was rubbing his hip raw, but he was happy. Dickie was behind him sweating.

Though they followed the stream up a deep, narrowing valley, the high, early afternoon sun found them, beat on their necks, and reflecting from the water, blinded them. As the path reversed the stream's descent, it became rougher, and when the steep banks finally gave them shadow, limestone rocks and roots protruded from the path, and they had to watch closely where they stepped.

"How far?" Dickie panted.

"Can't remember for sure. A ways though." Mark paused long enough to wipe the sweat from his eyes, smiled to himself, and ground on. Moss-covered boulders the size of houses, some large enough to have trees growing on them, tilted at crazy angles from the hillside, leaned over the path, and blocking any cooling breezes, held the air close and heavy in their shadows. Beside them the stream plunged noisily, turning back on itself as it tumbled from pool to pool, dashing against wedges of rock as it ran sharp and swift from its source.

The path climbed relentlessly. Mark, strong in his spitefulness, drove his body to punish Dickie. Seeing the rise that led shortly to the campsite, he increased the pace. Dickie begged for a break. The path veered sharply between two large boulders. "Not far now," Mark said and stepped through the opening. He was leaning, propped against the rock when Dickie plodded through.

"This is it," Mark said.

"Bout time," Dickie grumbled without looking up. He dropped his pack at his feet and found himself gazing into a deep pool. He raised his eyes, surveying the surface, following its length forty or fifty feet to where a small waterfall splashed into it. Plunging down, a white froth, the water veiled a dark cliff face. Trees leaned precariously from its top, their roots dangling like a fringe of unkempt hair through its edge. He dropped his eyes and saw he was standing on a long shelf of rock bound on one side by the pool and on the other by a wall of boulders. Along the boulders he saw the remnants of many past camps. Log benches, flattened on one side and wedged solid with stones, formed a semicircle to his right. In its center, a shallow firepit scraped out of the rock was black with the coals of ceremonial fires.

"Kitchen's over there," Mark said, pointing beyond the benches to an open space pocked with the scars of small cooking fires and rimmed with tables made of saplings lashed together with binder twine. "The sleeping area is just past it. Latrine is around behind the boulders."

"Not bad," Dickie pronounced as if he had made it. "Think I'll stay."

Mark stepped over the benches and hung his pack from a stake that had been driven into a crack in one of the boulders. Gesturing to another peg, he said, "Hang yours there, we've got work to do."

"Nuts!" Dickie answered. "I'm not doing nothin until I cool off." He skinned off his shirt, and balancing first on one foot and then the other, removed his shoes and socks, and pulled off his pants. Naked, standing pale and vulnerable in the shadow at the edge of the water, he looked small and diminished to Mark. He poised to dive.

"You'll freeze your butt," Mark warned, but he had waited until Dickie had launched himself in the air. He arched high and cut cleanly through the dark surface into the cold depths. He turned quickly and kicked off the bottom. When his head broke the surface, his voice erupted in a cry of pain and surprise. He threw his hands above his head, gasped in a shock of air, and went under. Mark watched the white body sink slowly, writhe, swim two froglike strokes towards shore, and then push off hard. It shot, a pale, flashing scar across the black depth and emerged, a long shrivel-skinned arm and blue-lipped face at his feet. He reached down, grabbed the hand, and hauled Dickie onto the shore.

"Gimme a towel," Dickie said.

"Didn't bring one."

"That water's cold!"

"Forty-eight degrees. Swimming the pool is a scout initiation ordeal."

"Yeah? Well, how does a scout thaw his butt?"

"He climbs the kitchen boulder and lays in the sun."

Dickie turned away, embraced the rock, and started climbing. Watching him, Mark remembered the day of his initiation. He had been twelve. Unlike Dickie, he had known the water was cold. It had been described to him in detail, and he had stood at its edge paralyzed while the troop goaded and jeered. When he finally dove, he had tried to catch himself at the last moment and had ended up bellyflopping, losing the momentum of the dive that should have carried him nearly across the pool. So his passage had been chillingly slow. He had climbed out shivering uncontrollably, and Mr. Delaney had thrown a rough wool blanket around him. He remembered the coarse scratch of its rub against his body as he huddled in it before throwing it off to climb the rock to the sunlight warmth of its flat top. There he had lain, his eyes closed, his body stretched out soft on the hard rock, and awash in sensation, he had fallen asleep. When he had awakened, he was glad he had been alone. He wondered if Dickie, halfway up the rock, felt anything like he had felt. But he doubted it, and he didn't ask. He turned instead to making camp.

4

Camp

A pair of posts joined by a crossbar had been erected near the boulder wall. Mark dug a canvas from his pack and attached it to the crossbar. Then, stringing the remaining tie ropes through rings pegged to the stone, he pulled it taut and tied it off, making a shelter. Leaving the campsite, he hiked a short way up the trail to a pine grove and cut a large armload of small branches. He hauled them back, knelt under the canvas, and wove a thick mattress for himself. Rolling his sleeping bag out, he glowed with satisfaction, for Mr. Delaney never let his scouts cut pine boughs. "You'd have the whole woods down, if I'd let you," he'd always say, laughing. So every time he'd been here before Mark had obediently scraped out a hip hole and had tossed, nearly sleepless on the uncomfortable rock, all night. "Not tonight," he said to himself.

He collected a handful of twigs and set up a small teepee in one of the kitchen fire rings. Beside it he placed larger sticks and finally a few small logs. He soaked the teepee with charcoal lighter and touched it off. As it burned, he arranged his cook kit and opened the two cans of Dinty Moore stew he'd packed in for supper. When he'd fed the fire and built a hot bed of coals, he set the coffee pot in them, hung the stew pot over them, and lay back to wait. Getting up occasionally to stir the stew, he let it simmer far longer than necessary, prolonging his private order. He was glad Dickie had been too impatient to set up camp before swimming the pool. He preferred to work without talking, and if Dickie had been helping, he would have had to talk, and talk would have spoiled the luxury of doing everything his own way. At last, he admitted he could delay no longer. He stood, called Dickie, and from the fireside watched his descent. Spread stretched from hand to toehold against the dark stone, Dickie looked remarkably like an albino lizard, and Mark wondered that some great beaked bird did not swoop from the sky, pluck him from the rock, and soar off to a nest of hungry fledglings. Safe on the ground, Dickie dressed, and in silence they ate overflowing platefuls of stew, mopping up the gravy with soft, white bread, stuffing it, a slice at a time, into their mouths. When they finished, they rinsed their dishes in the stream, and Dickie dug several old blankets from his pack and started to lay out a bed.

"No mattress?" Mark asked.

"Naw, I can sleep anywhere." As if to prove his point, he stretched out on his back, fumbled in his shirt pocket for his cigarettes and matches, and lit up. "Want one?" he asked, tossing the pack to Mark.

Mark picked up the pack and lay back on his mattress. The boughs crushed under his weight, releasing their light fragrance. Mark breathed it in, considered the cigarettes in his hand, and set them aside.

"This is the life," he said.

Three smoke rings but no words rose from Dickie's mouth.

Mark turned to watch the fire. Then, restless, unable to tolerate the silence, he got his carbide lamp. He unscrewed the reservoir, took it to the stream and filled it with water. He returned, screwed it back on, and wrinkling his forehead with excessive concentration, adjusted the drip. He opened the aperture in the middle of the reflector, smiled at the gentle hiss, and lit it. A wild flame flared at his fingers, shooting a surprising beam of light into the dusk settling on the camp. He reduced the flow of gas, and the flame shrank to an invisible core of brightness in the center of the lamp.

"Perfect," he said.

Dickie roused himself. "What's it like in the cave?" he asked.

"Dark."

"I know that."

"No you don't. It's dark like nothing you've ever imagined. The first time I was here Mr. Delaney got us all the way in, as far from the entrance as we could go, and then he made us blow out our lights. It was so black I held my hand up. I felt my breath blowing back in my face from it, but I couldn't see it. Then it seemed to get hot. I felt as if I were inside something alive and it was going to start squeezing. I don't know what I woulda done if another kid hadn't started screaming.

"Mr. Delaney got his light on fast, but it didn't do much good. The kid kept bawling. He cried the whole way out. We had to beg and bully to get him to crawl through the tunnels, and once he was out, he wouldn't go back in."

"It scare you?"

"I can't say."

"Bull."

"No. Scared's the wrong word. It's not strong enough. And it's too strong. I remember when I was twelve, I had to join church." Mark looked away and talked to the dark. "I had to take all those classes, and then they had a special service where we all took communion for the first time. Most of the kids were real serious. But next to me these two were snickering and asking for seconds. It was lousy bread cut up in little squares and Welch's grape juice for God's sake! And I was watching Rachel Cook. She was all breathy with phony emotion, and her bazoos kept rising up under her blouse. I wanted to lean over and touch them. Then I felt crap-awful. I was supposed to be praying. And all I had was this bitter taste in my mouth from the juice."

Mark paused and turned towards Dickie.

"I did once," Dickie said.

Not following, Mark asked, "Did what?"

"Touched her bazoos."

Mark flushed and refused to offer the leading question Dickie was waiting for. The night squeezed his chest. He hated Dickie, and he hated Dickie's experience. He hated himself, and he hated his innocent blundering into such revealing confessions. He turned and fiddled with his lamp.

"You ever blow up a can with one of these?" he asked.

Dickie shook his head.

Mark moved away from the fire and poured a small cone of carbide on the ground. He drew a thin line from it with his knife, then dripped a small amount of water onto the cone, placed the stew can over it, and stepped back. He counted to twenty while the gas built, struck a match, and laid it at the end of the carbide line. A small flame dashed towards the can and disappeared.

A yellow flash, like a low lightning bolt, leapt from the ground. A loud kawumph echoed through the camp, and the can blew into the night, ripping through the trees at the cliff top, and settling with a quiet clunk somewhere up the hill.

5
Morning

Sunday morning Tom Baker got up, pulled on a faded red terrycloth robe, and shuffled to the bathroom. The grim face that blankly returned his gaze from the mirror promised nothing, so he left it. He showered briefly, shut off the water while he soaped, and then rinsed, gradually easing the lever towards the cold. When he could stand it no longer, he snapped it off and toweled briskly. The face in the mirror came alive. It needed shaving.

He took his shaving kit from the medicine chest and arranged it on the sink before him. Humming he screwed the handle and head of his razor together.

"Rock of ages cleft for me."

He unwrapped a thin Gillette blue blade and slipped it into place.

"Let me hide myself in thee.
"Let the water and the blood."

He stopped. "Not very good words to shave to," he said to his face in the mirror. "Better try something else."

He ran scalding water, wet his brush, and began to work the soap in his shaving mug into a lather. As he swirled the brush, he broke out boisterously, "We have heard the joyful sound," but he caught himself before he could bellow, "Jesus shaves! Jesus shaves!" and, dropping his voice, he switched tunes again.

"Nothing but the blood of Jesus."

He raised his eyes to the mirror and began applying the lather. *I've got blood on my mind this morning*, he thought, and then he remembered it was communion Sunday. The words of the service came to him, and he said them over softly, "This cup is the new testament in my blood: this do ye, as oft as ye drink it, in remembrance of me." Sobered, he twisted his face to one side and thoughtfully drew the razor down his tightened cheek. Lather and beard came off smoothly. He shaved the other cheek and then raised his head to pull the skin of his neck taut. He drew the razor up around his chin, neatly removing his heaviest beard. He did not cut himself until he did his upper lip. There the dulled blade snagged and nipped, sending a trickle of blood into his mouth. He wiped it away, held the washcloth to it for a moment, and left the bathroom with a small piece of toilet paper dried to his face.

* * *

Mark woke early. Gray light filled the bowl of the campsite. He lay looking up into the blank expanse of canvas over his head.

Sunday, he thought. He closed his eyes and lay back.

During the night, his mattress had crushed, and Mark could feel not only the rock beneath him but the broken branches themselves. He sat up and slid from the sleeping bag. He unrolled his shoes from his jeans, which had been his pillow, and dressed. Without waking Dickie, he built a fire and put the coffee on. Leaving it to heat, he walked towards the stream. He stopped short of the water and stood back watching for movement. First he saw minnows in the shallows. Then as his eyes learned the bottom, he saw the small finning of trout holding themselves steady along the line between the still water and the current. He smiled and slipped cautiously back to his rucksack.

When he returned to the stream, he went to the foot of the pool and, balancing on protruding stones, made his way to the middle. A few feet above him, the trout held their places. He glanced back, assured himself Dickie was still asleep, and took a cherry bomb from his pocket. He lit it, held it at arm's length until the last second, and then flipped it over the pool above the trout. The crash exploded back and forth in the grotto. A geyser rose from the water. And Dickie, erupting from sleep, cried, "What the hell!"

Two trout, their speckled sides to the light, floated to Mark. Doubled with laughter, he bent over, lifted them from the water, raised them to Dickie's sight, and called, "Come eat."

Back on shore he gutted the fish, pulled the gills out, rinsed them in the stream, and carried them to the fire. He coated them with butter, wrapped them in foil, laid the packets at the edge of the fire, and raked the coals over them.

He poured two cups of coffee, gave one to Dickie, and they sat sipping while the fish baked. He didn't burn them, and when he unrolled them, they ate them from the foil, butter dripping from their chins and fingers.

* * *

The church parking lot was half filled when Tom turned from the street. He drove slowly to the end of the row and pulled to a stop.

"It's good not to have to hurry," he said.

Nancy heard the impatience in his voice and answered his unspoken thought. "Mark never means to make us late."

Tom glanced quickly at her, then spoke out the window. "I didn't say that."

"You didn't have to," she said. "Look here a second."

"What?"

"Are you planning to wear that toilet paper all day?"

Tom rubbed his hand under his nose. "I forgot," he said.

"What else have you forgotten?" Nancy laughed.

"That you can read minds."

"Then I was right?"

"It's easier when it's just us."

"I worry sometimes. You need to talk to him more."

Tom stiffened and reached for the door handle. "We'll be late," he said. He pushed his door open, swung his legs out, and stood up. A car squeezing into a small space nearer the church caught his eye, and he squinted at the driver. He twisted around, then ducked his head back into the car. "You said Mark was off with Delaney."

"Yes. They're at the cave."

"Delaney just pulled in," he said, a cold, deliberate control underscoring the sudden anger in his voice. He straightened, slammed the door, and started across the lot.

Nancy jumped from the car. "Wait!" she called, hurrying after him. When he stopped, she spoke softly, "Not now. After church."

He nodded, and they went inside.

At the beginning of his sermon, Reverend Hunt stood silently, gripping the sides of the pulpit, and waited for a deepening quiet to settle on the congregation. When he spoke, he spoke softly, his intimate bass reaching from the platform to bring each listener close to his words.

"On the night that he was betrayed our Lord Jesus took bread, and blessed it, and brake it, and gave it to the disciples, and said, 'Take, eat; this is my body.'

"And he took the cup, and gave thanks, and gave it to them, saying, 'Drink ye all of it; for this is my blood shed for the remission of sins.'

"These words from the gospel of Matthew, so well known to each of us, come easily to my lips. I learned them as a child. I heard them as a young man. I studied them in seminary. And I have said them every time I have celebrated communion since my ordination. I have, in fact, spoken them so often that I have almost forgotten the joy I felt the first time I said them in a service."

He paused, waited for the congregation to accept his confession, and then brought them into it.

"I wonder if you haven't forgotten also."

Seeing them stir, he raised his voice slightly.

"Let us consider a new text. The gospel of John, chapter 21.

"Christ has been betrayed.

"He has sweat blood in the garden.

"He has been mocked, scourged, and spat upon.

"He has been abandoned by his disciples.

"He has been crucified.

"He has died and lain three days in the grave.

"And he has risen from the dead.

"But he has not yet ascended into Heaven. He has shown himself to the disciples, but as usual they are confused. Peter has decided to go fishing. Thomas, Nathanael, James, John, and two others have followed him. They have fished all night and caught nothing. But it's not been for want of trying. Peter has been working so hard he has stripped for comfort and is naked. In the morning a man calls to them from the shore.

"'Any luck?' he cries.

"'None,' Peter answers.

"'Try the other side of the boat,' the man hollers.

"Agreeable, like any modern fisherman, to one more cast, Peter tries the other side of the boat. He nets so many fish, he can't haul them in. Suddenly the situation looks familiar to John.

"'It is the Lord,' he says.

"Peter, demonstrating once again that he had a rock for a brain, pulls on his coat and jumps in the water. The other disciples bring in the boat and the catch.

"Let us begin reading now at verse 9. 'As soon then as they were come to land, they saw a fire of coals there, and fish laid thereon, and bread. Jesus saith unto them, "Bring of the fish which ye have now caught" . . . and

Jesus saith unto them, "Come and dine" . . . Jesus then cometh, and taketh bread, and giveth them, and fish likewise.'

"I have always regarded this passage as a kind of afterthought to the main business of Saint John's gospel. I have thought John tucked it in to give us a hint about the nature of the resurrected body, to remind us that the resurrection is not merely spiritual. The passage, indeed, does that, but I realize now it does much more.

"Imagine with me that morning beside the sea of Galilee. Peter is dripping wet. The other disciples are amused. They tease, 'That freshened the air.'

"'Yeah, but it left us the nets.'

"'Watch out, the water flies when he shakes.'

"And I can hear Jesus chuckling. He is poised beside the fire, tending the coals. 'Hurry up and clean those fish,' he says.

"Nathanael grins, 'I've got one done, can't you multiply it?'

"'Clean the fish,' Jesus answers. Their laughter breaks like waves over the water. Seven tired, hungry fishermen are rejoicing, as boisterous, hardworking men rejoice, in the company of their Lord. And he is rejoicing with them. At last he takes bread, and he takes the fish. He holds them out and he says, 'Come. Eat.' He says no more, for thick as they often are, they understand. Jesus is once again inviting them to a feast. This time, however, there are no undertones of mystery, no hints of suffering, no anguish. This time it is clear. The Lord's breakfast is a celebration of his resurrection and their salvation. They eat and they are filled.

"My people. As we gather at this table, we must acknowledge that, like the disciples, we have betrayed Christ. We have slept in the garden. And we have run from his accusers. But we must also, like the disciples, recognize that that is in the past. Christ has come back for us. He calls us from the shore.

" 'Try the other side of the boat.'

" 'Bring me the fish you have caught.'

" 'Come. Eat.' "

As the elders went forward to serve the elements, Tom Baker thought of Mark. Mark had certainly lied to Nancy. Bob Delaney was in church. The scouts were not camping. Was Mark? Probably. And he was probably at Lemon Hole. He wasn't stupid. Though he would lie to get away, he'd make sure someone knew where he was. The question he faced was, What should he do?

He set it aside to watch the plate of bread being passed down the aisle. When it reached him, he took it from his wife, brushing her hand by accident. The touch of her flesh at the moment he lifted the bread, the body of Christ, from the plate, shocked him into deeper thought. He held the bread in his fingers and worked it into a small ball. After his death, Christ did not judge his disciples for their fear, for their betrayals; he sought them out and fed them.

"This is my body, broken for you," the minister said. Tom raised his hand to his mouth and ate. The bland bread filled him. The anger he had felt in the parking lot passed, and he whispered to Nancy, "I'm glad you made me wait to see Delaney."

"Shh," she answered. "After."

He smiled. "That's what I'm saying."

She frowned and turned to receive the cup from her neighbor.

Tom accepted it from her and sat staring into the dark juice. By slowly swirling it he could catch the light from the ceiling and turn the liquid gold. But he could not keep it gold. The surface, in motion, kept turning back to purple, reminding him that he held not only the blood of Christ, but grape juice. And it came to him that Christ was in his flesh, just as surely as he was in the juice. If he could stay in the light, he would be transformed. The alchemist dream would be true, only something of infinitely more value than a gross shining metal was being made; a man was being taken up into God's flesh without leaving the world. Absorbed in his thoughts, he raised the cup and drank. Then he heard the order, "Drink ye all of it," and he looked around, vaguely guilty, but grinning as the rest of the congregation drank. Smiling broadly, he stood when the hymn was announced and sang,

> But drops of grief can ne'er repay
> The debt of love I owe:
> Here, Lord, I give myself away—
> 'Tis all that I can do.

After the benediction, he turned to his wife and said, "Be right back."

She stopped him with a hand on his arm and a soft, "Wait."

"I'm not angry," he said. "But Mark needs to come home. I'm going to get Bob Delaney and then go for him."

6

Lemon Hole

They had no map, but on previous trips, exploring with the scout troop, Mark had learned the name of every obstacle and had memorized every turn. Kneeling at the entrance, a rope looped over his shoulder, his lamp lighted and attached to his cap, Mark knew the caving should be easy. Only two dangerous descents awaited, and he had done both many times. Still he felt unsure. He stole a furtive look at the sky, swallowed, and crawled into the dark, his lamp illuminating a small, yellow circle ahead of him. The passage was wide, three feet high with plenty of clearance. He crawled quickly, scuffing his hands and knees on the cold, sandstone grit, and reached the first descent, a forty-foot drop down a narrow crevice, before Dickie's shadow darkened the opening of light behind him. For a moment he was alone. At the bottom of the crevice he saw his mother's face. Her hair had come undone, and she had not bothered to fix it. Her eyes were puzzled, and stared up at him brimming with disappointment. When he heard Dickie scrabbling in the tunnel, he turned away. When he looked back, he saw only stone. Then Dickie knelt beside him.

A log had been braced across the crevice. Mark knotted his rope around it, held the coils over the opening, and dropped them. They slithered uncoiling against the sides of the crack and plopped, plenty long, on the floor below. "This descent is called the Devil's Swing," he said. "You grab the rope, wrap your legs around it, and slide down. It's called the Swing because you drop through the roof of a cavern and do the last twenty feet twisting free on the rope. He lay over the log, hung his feet in the crevice, and eased down until he could grip the rope. "By the way," he said, "keep your head away from the rope. One kid set it afire with his lamp."

Mark raised his head, catching Dickie's face in his light. He saw what he wanted to see, the white complexion of fear, and he was glad. He lowered his head and gave his weight to his arms. "Don't wet your pants," he said over his shoulder and disappeared. The rope, harsh in his palms, felt good, and he dropped hand over hand, cocooned in the globe of light about his head. While his shoulders still bumped against the sides of the crevice, he felt his legs and hips slip free into air. He gripped the rope tightly and held himself steady. Then slowly he let himself down through the ceiling, and climbed without swinging to the floor of the cavernous room.

"Your turn!" he yelled. "I'll hold the rope tight."

"Let it swing!"

Dickie came down recklessly, too fast, sliding, the rope burning his hands. When he slipped below the crevice, he swung wildly, banged his head, swore, hung on with one hand, and grabbed at the ceiling with the other. He stabilized himself momentarily, started slipping again, lost the rope with his feet, slid several feet, let go, and dropped to the floor. He hit, stumbled, and ended sitting at Mark's feet.

"Nice slide," Mark said.

Dickie hauled himself up. "Piece of cake. Where do we go from here?"

"Listen."

At first Dickie could hear only the hissing of the lamps. Then under it he heard running water, and finally under that he heard an occasional faint rustle, as if a sheet were being shifted on a bed.

"What is it?" he asked.

"Bats. The roof is crawling with them." Watching Dickie, Mark picked his words carefully. "If we had a stronger light you could see. There are so many, when they move, it looks like the cave itself breathes."

"What's this on the floor?"

Mark grinned. "You get one guess."

"Which way outa here?"

"Over there through Fat Man's Misery. Suck your gut in and edge sideways. After that it's an easy walk downhill. Dickie followed Mark through the narrow crack in the wall and stepped out into a wide, high-arched corridor that sloped sharply away into the dark. In the center of it, a tiny trickle of water cut into the stone. Mark led the way along it. Where the corridor leveled, the stream widened into a shallow pool and ended. Mark sat, leaned over it and shone his light into the water. He motioned Dickie to join him and pointed. Small colorless fish swam oblivious to the sudden brightness. "They're blind," he said. "Since they live in the dark, they don't need eyes."

"Weird. Whata they eat?"

"Not much. Probably microscopic stuff. They don't get very big."

For several minutes they sat in the eerie glow of their lamps. The cold, alien life of the pale fish swam incomprehensibly before them. Their light, reflected from the water, hit the dull walls and died, and the circle of warmth about them seemed to shrink. More out of need than calculation Mark spoke. "You wanta lead awhile?"

"I don't know the way."

"The turns are all marked. Watch."

Mark took his lamp from his cap and held it to the wall. When he moved it away, a black carbon smear remained. He held it close again and wrote his name. "Follow the arrows."

"Can I trust them?"

"I'll know if they're wrong, but they won't be. Start down that tunnel there."

"Right."

A few minutes later, Mark was squirming through a passage barely wide enough for his shoulders. Though he'd been down it before and knew it widened, he remembered the stories of men crawling into tight places and getting stuck, and he thought with certain delight what Dickie was thinking as he wormed ahead ignorant of every turn until he came to it. Sweating, Mark lay still to rest. Though Dickie was out of sight around a bend, Mark could hear him panting and grunting as he scrunched along the rock. *Keep going,* he thought, and he removed his cap and lamp and set them ahead of him.

Mark liked being alone in the tunnel. He liked the damp that was neither cool nor warm. He liked the slow sense of the walls closing in as he lay silently, the coarse grit of the walls and floor against his skin. He liked feeling himself turning to stone and then, in the moment before panic turned him rigid, starting to crawl forward, pulling himself by his elbows deeper and deeper into the earth, further and further from the burning light of the sun.

He reached his lamp, held it steady on the floor, and turned the gas down. The flame, darting from the reflector like a tongue, withdrew. His eyes held the light, a glowing afterimage. It faded, and like a blind fish he swam into the icy depths of the dark. He drifted in the current a long time, then he rose, and floated in the stone. At last, as if awakening, he realized he no longer swam in silence. A voice calling his name from a great distance wound about him. He resisted it, but it came again, and he answered.

He worked his left arm between the wall and his body, found his pocket, and dug a pack of matches from it. He struck one and by its small flickering light found his lamp, but it burned down quickly. He snuffed it out as it bit at his fingers, and lit another one. He turned the gas up on his lamp, and as he moved the match towards the aperture in the center of the reflector, the flicker bloomed and then burst.

He snugged his cap on his head, fixed the light to it, and hunched forward. The tunnel, which moments before had felt as roomy as the ocean, closed in. Hurrying he dug his elbows into the stone and lifted himself ahead. He pushed with his knees and scraped the sides. The tunnel opened, and he rose to his hands and knees. Crawling quickly, pausing at forks only long enough to make sure of the arrows, he heaved himself forward, his breath pounding in his chest, until Dickie's voice grew loud with nearness. Then he slowed. As his breathing settled into a quiet rhythm, he heard the splash of falling water, and he emerged from the tunnel into a small dome-shaped room. Beside him the stream poured from an opening in the wall and spilled onto the floor. It gathered itself and flowed across the room slipping between two rounded hassock-sized formations, then disappeared over the edge of a steep, scree-covered slope opening underneath a low overhang in the far wall. Dickie sat before him on one of the stone mounds.

"Comfortable?" Mark asked. He stepped over the stream, and eased himself down on the other mound.

"Yeah. What took you so long?"

"Everybody I know who's been in this room's sat on these." He watched Dickie absently stroking the smooth surface of the rock. "This room's called Aphrodite's Bath."

"Whose?"

"Aphrodite. Remember? From history."

"No."

"The Greek goddess of love. We're sitting on her boobs."

Dickie jerked his hand from the stone and grasped his knee. "People who name these places, you know, they gotta be a little sick."

"Ain't everybody?"

"I ain't."

Mark started to answer but stopped. The light from

his lamp lay on Dickie's face, softening it, turning it almost girlish and innocent, and suddenly Mark understood. Dickie was right; uncompromisingly at ease with his flesh, ready to take whatever would yield to his will, he had no need to make snickering jests about stone boobs to contain the wildness of his urges. He was a totally natural man.

"I guess you aren't," Mark said. Shamed by the awareness of his own sickness churning in him like food poisoning, Mark shifted his eyes to avoid Dickie's. He looked past him to the wall, and there he saw the grim, distorted shadow of Dickie's body, twisting in the flickering light, bestial against the dark stone.

"We gonna sit here all day?" Dickie asked.

"We go down the slope under that overhang," Mark said. "It's called Skid Row. The deepest point of the cave is at the bottom."

"Then we climb back up?"

"We could, but we'd miss a lot of cave. Another set of tunnels leads back to the Devil's Swing. That climb we can't avoid."

"Let's go." Dickie stood, stepped across the room, and bent to duck under the overhang.

"Hold on!" Mark ordered. "This is where we use the second rope. Can we leave it, or do you wanna sneak it back onto the truck?"

"Probably ought to."

"Okay. I'll anchor this end for you. Then when you're down, I'll loop it around Aphrodite, and you can anchor me from the bottom."

Mark divided the coils and threw about half onto the scree. "That oughta do," he said. He sat down and arranged the rope so it ran from the coil around his back and then down the slope. He grabbed the rope on each side of his body and nodded to Dickie, "Ready when you are."

Holding lightly, flexing his fingers, he waited as Dickie, stooped low, picked up the rope, and inched under the rock. He watched him try to back, half standing, down the scree, saw his feet start to go, gripped tightly, and caught the shock of Dickie's weight as he sprawled on his face in the wet stones. He held it easily. "Careful," he called. "The only way to go is to slide on your belly."

"Shove it," Dickie answered.

Mark felt the rope go slack as Dickie raised himself to his feet, then felt it tighten as he crab-stepped backwards. Dickie's weight jarred him again, and he laughed, "Give it up." Dickie didn't answer but the repeated small bumps against his back told Mark he was sliding hand over hand. Then they stopped.

"I'm at the end of the rope," Dickie yelled.

"Hang on! I'll let you down."

Mark tried to feed the rope out gently, but Dickie pulled heavily, and it slipped through his hands. It burned, and he squeezed, stopping the run.

"Listen," he hollered. "We did this wrong. There's a drop-off at the end of that slope, and I don't think I can let you over it. I've got to feed you enough rope to reach the bottom, so you can climb."

"Fine time to tell me."

"Sorry. Lay out flat so you don't slide. Say when and I'll let go of the rope and you can pull it past you."

"Ready."

Mark let go of the rope. It uncoiled and slid in short jerks across the floor and down the slope. He leaned back, stretched, and rolled his shoulders to relax them. Suddenly his name sounded over the loud clatter and scrape of sliding stones. He straightened. The rope leapt away from him along the floor. He grabbed at it, but his stiff fingers would not close.

"Dickie!" he screamed, and flung himself at its writhing.

In the long instant of his panic, he did not feel the stone crush his mouth. Nor did he see his lamp, spewing light, fly wildly from his head and crash against the floor. He tasted only the warm saltiness of blood streaming from his torn lip, and he cried, "Oh, sweet Jesus."

In darkness the cold rock bruised his cheek. Silence answered his cry. And he knew he was lost. Without moving he called, "Dickie." He listened but heard no sounds rise from the bottom. Jumping suddenly to sit up, he banged his head on the overhang. Red swirls spun in his eyes, and he knelt half sick, until they stopped.

Trembling, he groped in his pocket for his matches, found them, and struck one. By its light he crawled to his lamp which had fallen near the stream. The reflector was bent, and the reservoir had spilled, so he set a burning match on the floor, and twisted the lamp apart. The match went out as he refilled the reservoir, and he fumbled in the dark. When he felt the lamp fit together, he screwed it tight, struck another match, and touched it to the hissing gas. Light leapt to the walls and opened the room for Mark to act.

Deliberately he tied the rope to one of the mounds. Then he flattened himself on the muddy scree and worked his way carefully to the drop-off. He edged his feet over it, wrapped them about the rope, and shinnied down, his knees, arms, and face scraping against the stone. When he reached the bottom, he turned quickly.

His light swept over Dickie who lay on his back, one leg bent under him, on a pile of loose stones, and came to rest on his face. Half seeing, Mark watched Dickie's eyes open, stare into the light, and slowly focus.

A dry, frightened voice croaked at him, "Help me sit."

As if waking, he knelt at Dickie's head, cradled it under an arm, and lifted, but Dickie cried out, "Oh! No!" He stretched out an arm and gestured towards his leg.

Mark eased him back down and, following the gesture, reached tentatively to touch Dickie, but he held his fingers inches away, and glanced back to Dickie's face.

"You gotta look," he said.

Mark felt Dickie cringe when his hand touched the leg. He drew a deep breath, grasped the pantleg, and gently pulled it back. When it cleared the wound, he turned, his face drained of expression, back to Dickie's eyes. Reflected in the lamplight, they were the eyes of a small spellbound animal.

"Is it bad, Mark?"

"It's broken. The bone's sticking out."

"It hurts to move."

"Don't even try. Moving will only make it worse."

"How do we get out of here?"

"I don't know," Mark answered.

"You gotta leave me."

"It'll be hours. Can you take it?"

"Do I have a choice?"

Mark looked around the room and saw only stones. "There's nothing here for a splint," he said. Then he mused, "From here back to the swing, the cave is mostly good sloping tunnel. If I tied your legs together, I could probably get you back to the entrance, but it'd be hell, and I doubt if I could pull you out alone."

Dickie laughed grimly, "Like I said. Do I have a choice?"

Mark stood and searched the room until he found Dickie's lamp. Then he sat, propping himself against the wall. "I'll fix this for you," he said.

"How long will it last?"

"A couple hours."

Though Dickie said nothing, Mark could see he was calculating the time it'd taken them to get from their campsite to the cave and then to its bottom. He set Dickie's lamp beside him and stood. When he said nothing, Dickie spoke.

"I'm sorry I screwed up."

Stunned, Mark crossed the room. At the tunnel entrance, he stopped and turned back to Dickie, "You know, I was pushing you. I wanted the cave to beat you." He paused, waiting for forgiveness. But Dickie said nothing and shadows hid his face. Mark stepped towards him. "I didn't want anything like this," he said.

"It's okay. Go." Dickie dismissed him, and he went.

7

I'm Not Alone

The tunnel that ran most directly from the cavern below Skid Row to the foot of the Devil's Swing sloped steadily upward. Hunched over, leaning into it, Mark almost ran. His steps, hitting heavily, heaving him forward, bounced his light crazily up from the floor, over the walls, and off the ceiling. Kaleidoscopic patterns of stone and color changed before him, and he plunged through them without seeing his way. The steepness, however, wore on him, and gradually, his breath coming in short gasps, he slowed to a walk. His breathing fell into a steady rhythm and the whirling patterns settled into a single probe of light stretching before him towards hope. He followed it as if it were a fiery pillar and not a beam originating from the lamp on his hat.

When the probe narrowed, funneled by the floor, walls, and ceiling coming together, he bent double and continued. When he scraped his back, he dropped to his hands and knees and crawled without slowing, but the stones pounded him, tore the skin from his hands, and ripped at his knees. He grew hot, and realized he was wet with perspiration, but he drove on. The tunnel was longer than he remembered. It shrank. He went on his belly. Halfway through a tight twisting corner, he banged his head on a protruding rock, and suddenly he stopped. Knocked into awareness, he saw his bloody hands before him, felt the grip of the rock on his hips, and knew he had made a wrong turn. Utterly lost, he dropped his head to his extended arms and wept.

When he had exhausted his grief, he backed down the tunnel until he reached a point where he could sit up. He sat, scrunched himself into a ball and worked himself around. Then he crawled until he could stand. He went slowly downhill, descending into renewed fear, searching for the carbide arrows that would lead him out. At last he found one. Following it, he started to ascend. He found another and another. With each rising step he felt stronger, more ready to meet the end he could neither avoid nor desire. Upright he came into a large cavern and heard the rustle of bats hanging from the ceiling. In the center of the room he found his rope, took it in his hands, and looked up the Devil's Swing.

Ready to climb, he shifted his hands high above his head, and jumping to wrap his knees about the rope, squeezed tightly. The rough fibers of the hemp stung his raw palms like a thousand needles as his hands closed, and he fell with a surprised howl to the floor. He picked himself up. Once again, this time steeling himself, he gripped the rope and lifted his weight. It was impossible. The stinging pain forced him to let go, and he stood at the end of the rope hopeless and broken.

"Help!" he screamed. The word bounced from the walls and fell dead. He sat and stared. The rope, tantalizing and near, dangled in front of him. Then he remembered, *Gloves. Mr. Delaney always made us wear gloves.* He stood, stripped off his shirt, and tried to rip it, but with his bleeding hands he could not tear through the seams. He cut them with his pocket knife. The shirt yielded, and he wrapped strips of cloth around his hands.

In his grip the rope remained a hard core of pain, but the cloth protected him from the cutting fibers. Slowly, hand over hand, the rope wound between his legs, he rose from the floor towards the narrow crevice in the roof. Sweat beaded on his forehead and ran into his eyes, blinding him, but he did not need to see. His hands, throbbing, cramped on the rope, focused his attention. They became him, and he spoke to himself. "Hang on," he said. "Oh God, help me hang on." And he held on. When he reached the crevice, he caught his shoulder on the ceiling and slid back. He clamped his legs hard and clutched the burning in his palms until it scored through him and came out a long piercing wail, and he stopped. Carefully he pulled himself into the crevice and without releasing the rope drew his knees up and wedged himself into place. As he felt his body settle against the walls and hold him, he loosed his grip and rested. Then, using his legs and scraping his back on the stone, he pressed himself upward.

Near the top, he rested again, and as his breathing quieted, he heard scraping above him and a voice saying, "There's a light showing."

"Who's there?" he called, and pressed hard against

the wall, lifting himself to reach for the log spanning the top.

"Mark?" the voice asked.

"Yes," he answered. "Help me." In the instant of his asking he felt strong hands grasp him by the armpits. He gave his weight to them and allowed them to pull him over the log onto the level floor, where exhaustion overwhelmed him. He lay trembling on his stomach, his face flat on the rock, and then, knowing that he was not yet free, that he would never be free, he turned to look into the awful, compassionate faces of his father and Mr. Delaney.

"I'm not alone," he said.

"Not now," his father answered.

"No. Dickie's with me. I left him at the bottom. He's hurt. Bad." He looked from his father to Mr. Delaney.

"Okay," Mr. Delaney said. "We'll get help."

Mark felt tears threatening. He raised a hand to wipe at his eyes and smeared his face with blood.

Part Three
1959

1

Mary

The last of his cross-country teammates had left, switching off the lights as he had gone, leaving Mark in near darkness. As he sat hunched before his open locker, wearing only his running shorts, the heavy locker-room air, a heady mixture of stale sweat and wintergreen liniment, settled on him like a blanket, and he felt like a sleeper resisting morning. He knew if he stirred, his dream, vague as it was, would end, and he wanted to stay, just a little longer, talking with Mary in the hall outside of her homeroom. But he did not want to hear what she was saying. He wanted to hear her saying the words he'd imagined before speaking himself. Half-conscious, he reached into his locker, hooked his flats with two fingers, and dumped them on the floor at his feet. He leaned over, staring at the damp socks tucked in them and watched for signs of life. When neither moved, he pulled one loose and passed it under his nose. Startled awake, he bent double to put it on and began to hurry. Before he could finish, the door banged, and he turned to see Dickie step into the room.

"You here, Mark?"

"No."

He faced his locker and concentrated on pulling his tee shirt right-side-out as Dickie crossed the room, his limp hidden by habit behind his clipboard. "Just keep quiet," Mark said when he heard the clipboard slap onto the bench beside him.

"Touchy," Dickie said.

"You said it."

"You see Mary?"

"Mind your own business."

"She turned you down."

"I didn't say that."

"So what did she say?"

"She wants me to go out with her."

"Then she's goin?"

"No. She wants me to go to some church party with her friends."

"Oh well, Peanut's always free."

Mark ducked his head into his tee shirt, avoiding Dickie's grin, and took his sweats from the locker. "I told her I'd go."

Dickie whistled. "What about tonight?"

Mark shrugged and kept his face to his locker. For a long moment they stood in silence. When Mark neither spoke nor moved to put on his sweats, Dickie picked up his clipboard and started towards the door. Halfway across the room he paused, looked back, and said, "A good girl will screw your mind."

"You know where you can go," Mark answered.

"Most likely," Dickie laughed, "but I'm going to practice first. You comin?"

"I'll catch up." Mark sat and draped his sweats across his legs. *Mary,* he thought. *Why does Mary sound so much like marry? At the party everyone was feeling Merry. The virgin merry. When Mary left, everybody.... Damn everybody and their horny minds.* He slammed the locker door, jerked his sweatpants over his shoes, and went out the door.

Stabbed suddenly by sunlight, he stopped and shielded his eyes. When they adjusted, he looked across the athletic field. Squat helmeted figures with pale, dirty legs protruding from tight, padded white pants huddled in bent-over groups. Others banged into blocking sleds or danced through a maze of old tires. Beyond them, near the oversized green scoreboard proclaiming, "Lamont Field: Home of the Oakland Owls," Dickie was starting down the path to the woods dividing the field from the meadow and the cross-country course. Defying angry whistles and barking yells, Mark dodged through the football practice, loped towards Dickie, and caught him at the edge of the woods.

2

Time Trial

"Better save some of that energy," Dickie said. Breathing easily, Mark snorted, "What for?"

"You forget? Time trial today."

"Big sweat," Mark answered.

"Coach expects a good time."

"So does Peanut."

"Go ahead, please," Dickie mimicked Coach Gale's voice starting a time trial.

Mark swatted the clipboard from Dickie's hand and ran circles around him as the papers scattered in the wind.

"Knock it off," Dickie snapped. He balanced awkwardly, his stiff leg lifting from the ground as he bent from the waist to gather the loose sheets. When one flipped away in the wind, Mark chased it down, snatching it up just before it blew into the woods. Suddenly he stopped and called, "Hey, look at this." Absorbed in ordering his papers, Dickie ignored him. Mark stooped and from the thick dry mat of fallen leaves, lifted a box turtle. It retracted its head, snapping the yellow-orange hinge of its shell shut, but it did not draw in its legs. Instead it flailed wildly, three kicking legs swimming futilely in the air. Mark turned it over, studied it, and carried it to Dickie, who still had not looked up. "It only has three legs," he said. "Must be tough humpin along."

"Tell me about it, hotshot," Dickie flared. He took the turtle and set it beside the path.

"Don't let it go," Mark protested. "It'll make a great mascot. Nothing in the world could be slower."

"Coach'll hate it."

"That's the point."

"And you'll expect me to carry it around, right?"

"Why not? It'd really be funny."

"You don't know nothin, do you?"

Mark looked down. Dickie followed his eyes to the turtle. Its heavy shell scored a thin line in the dust as it dragged itself into the protective leaves. Dickie pivoted and strode away, his body jerking ahead, rising on his stiff leg before pitching forward into each good step. When Mark looked up, the rhythmic hitch of Dickie's angry stride filled his vision. Embarrassment at the lithe fitness of his own body rose in him and he hated it. He nudged the turtle, tilting it upwards with his toe, and was about to kick it aside, when Coach Gale's voice interrupted him. "It's not a nature walk you're out for, Mark."

Caught, Mark blustered, "Look, Coach, a three-legged turtle. Wouldn't it make a great mascot?"

"No, Mark. I don't think it would. Come along."

When Mark and Coach Gale reached the field, the team was ready to go. Without stretching out, Mark quickly took a place at the end of the starting line away from the other varsity runners. Set, he looked down the long straightaway and grimaced. Even on good days he hated the near all-out sprint across the meadow to gain position before entering the narrow trail through the woods. He did not feel much like running, and when Coach Gale announced, "Go ahead, please," he did not break with the varsity. He crossed the field with the bunched pack of the second string, his arms bumping against his sides, his breath coming in arhythmic gasps, and the bitter taste of his lunch threatening his throat. At the turn downhill before the narrow gate into the woods which marked the first quarter mile, Dickie stood reading off times. Mark watched his feet, refusing to meet Dickie's eyes as he passed, but he could not refuse to hear the hissing voice, "89, 90, 91." Automatically he lengthened his stride as gravity took him and he pounded downhill through the gate.

The sudden shade felt good, but the spatter of light on the trail made him dizzy. He raised his eyes to the back of the man ten yards ahead. It was Baggs, the best of the younger runners, a half-coordinated, loud-voiced sophomore who too often forced himself into conversations and cliques. Mark knew he would soon challenge for a varsity spot and hated him for it. His flailing arms waved like turtle legs from the heavy shell of his back, and when he pitched sideways, thrown off stride by the unevenness of the trail, his awkward lurch to save himself from falling shocked Mark. For an instant he saw Dickie angrily stumping ahead of him, and his own anger broke into light. He concentrated on Baggs' back and felt his breathing settle. He lowered his arms and let them work freely at his sides. Relaxed, he picked up his pace.

He drew beside Baggs, but Baggs would not let him pass. Shoulder to shoulder they wound through the woods. Together they closed the distance between themselves and the varsity. Mark was annoyed. He wanted to swear at Baggs, to tell him to let off and run within himself, but he kept quiet. *Okay,* he thought, *if this is what you want, I'll run you into the ground.* At a tight corner at the bottom of a long hill, Mark forced Baggs to swing wide and take extra steps. They bumped, but Baggs did not fall back.

Mark shortened his stride for the uphill and leaned into the slope. "Stay with me, Baggs," he challenged. Baggs did. Together they caught the slowest of the varsity runners and passed him. Together they came out of the woods and bore down on the mile mark where Coach Gale read times. As he approached, Mark tensed, expecting sharp words. He heard only, "5:28, 5:29, 5:30," and as he swept by, "Good work, Baggs."

Fifty yards ahead, nearing the flag marking the turn at the mile and a quarter, he could see the leaders. "Come on, Baggs," he said. As he opened his stride, he felt quiet beside him. He glanced over his shoulder and saw Baggs a step behind him. He thought, *You're dead, hotshot,* but he said, "Come on. Let's get 'em." Baggs, gasping and pounding, determined to gut it out, moved up beside him. They bumped again at the flag where Mark, refusing to run wide, squeezed Baggs, and Baggs, between panting breaths, sputtered, "Sorry."

Mark sucked in a breath and almost tripped. A great

balloon of laughter swelled inside him. His lungs burned, pain stabbed at his side, and suddenly his anger was gone. *I'm trying to kill him,* he thought, *and all he hears is encouragement.* Stride for stride, in a tenuous harmony, they worked up the hill, Baggs wheezing and grunting, Mark moving effortlessly, lost in a kind of elation. He heard his voice sing-songing from somewhere far off, "Come on, Baggs. Come on, Baggs." And Baggs came on. At the crest, Mark tightened his stride to allow Baggs to swing around the corner beside him, and together they broke into a reckless plunge down the long, curving slope to the two-mile mark. When they reached it, only one runner, Simpson, the perennial number-two man on the team remained ahead of them.

Dickie was there with his stopwatch, "10:58, 10:59. Coach is smiling."

"A little more, Baggs," Mark urged.

But Baggs had no more. "Go," he gasped.

And Mark went. The course, looping once more into the woods, lay before him, and nothing else mattered, not even Simpson ahead. Mark ran the way he loved to run, alone, closed not into himself, but into a moving world of color, sound, and sensation. The earth rose up beneath his feet to receive him, gave as he came down, and lifted him forward as he pushed off. Thoughts rushed in his head. He knew all was restored, that Dickie would laugh at Baggs, that they'd forget about the turtle, that Saturday would come and the race would go well, and he wouldn't think anymore about Mary who was taking him to the party afterwards.

At the edge of the woods, he caught Simpson, but he did not try to pass him. He settled a stride behind and drafted, resting for the finishing sprint. Crossing the field, he matched Simpson stride for stride, gradually increasing speed as he felt Simpson straining to once more open a lead. Three hundred yards from the finish Simpson launched himself into a sprint. For a moment Mark did not respond. He watched the opening between them enlarge like the joy pounding in his chest. Then he started his kick. Easily, he closed the gap and drew beside Simpson. For two strides he ran on his shoulder. He felt him break, kicked harder and left him. At the finish he heard Coach Gale's voice, "14:02. Good finish, Mark."

He slowed to a jog and turned to see Baggs pounding, out of control, working his legs like pistons and his arms like windmills towards a spot on the varsity. He moved away as Baggs crossed the finish line, but Baggs, panting, ran straight to him.

"You were great, Mark. Thanks."

Embarrassed, Mark looked over Baggs' shoulder. "Here comes Coach," he said.

Baggs turned quickly, enthusiasm loosing his tongue, his speech plunging as wildly towards the ends of his sentences as his sprint had plunged towards the finish. "Coach, Mark was great. Did you see him pull me along? He never stopped talking to me. I couldn't believe it."

"That's all part of being a team, Albert. Remember it when you're first man."

As Baggs reveled in the gentle praise, Mark tried to slip away, but Coach Gale stopped him. "Walk back with me, Mark," he said. Mark nodded before turning away to walk a slow, looping circle to cool down. Then he sat to put on his sweats. As he sat, hugging his knees and rocking uneasily, Dickie came over to him. "Tonight still on?"

Mark stared at the ground. He thought of Peanut and

what a night along the creek with her might lead to. At the same time he thought of Mary. He looked up, but he said nothing.

Dickie dropped and sat beside him. "I'm in no hurry," he said.

"Coach wants me to walk with him," Mark answered.

"He liked what you did for Baggs." Dickie pushed himself up and started to leave.

"Wait," Mark said. "You still mad?"

Dickie turned slowly, "What about?"

"The turtle."

"Forget it. See you in the locker room." Dickie swung away, his limp almost lost in the quickness of his stride.

Mark rose slowly, sucked in his breath, and joined Coach Gale. As they left the meadow and entered the woods, Coach Gale spoke. "You don't like Albert, do you?"

Mark didn't answer.

"He's part of the team now. He made it because of you."

"I wasn't encouraging him."

"What were you doing?"

"I was trying to break him."

"And you couldn't."

"I don't know. When I realized he thought I was trying to help him, I thought how stupid he was, and I felt lousy trying to hurt him. Then I sorta wanted him to stay with me."

For a long time Coach Gale was silent. Mark knew he wasn't finished, so he waited, fearing what he might say next. When he spoke, as they came out of the woods, he seemed to change the subject. "Are you happy?"

Mark was surprised and puzzled. "About Baggs?"

"That will do for a start."

"No. He's a klutz, a big stupid dog who wants to sit on everyone's lap."

"But you did help him."

"Maybe I'm as stupid as he is."

"No." Coach paused. "I don't think you're stupid. I think sometimes you just can't stand being Mark."

"What's that mean?"

"It means, I think you're afraid of being the man you want to be."

Mark stopped. A feeling he could not name, a kind of cleansing anger beat in him like his heart coming down the stretch. He raised his eyes to meet Coach Gale's, and a determination not to choke held his voice back when he spoke. "And what do you think I want to be?"

Coach Gale met his eyes and did not turn away. "I think you want to be good."

Mark looked away. The football team was abandoning the field, dragging towards the locker room. He started to walk, as if to follow them, and said over his shoulder, "If I'm good, I'll be happy?"

Without moving, Coach Gale answered, "Happy was the wrong word. I should have said contented."

Mark turned, stepped back towards Coach, and glared. "You want something from me, don't you."

"I want something for you."

"What's that?"

"I want you to run with Baggs Saturday the way you ran with him today."

"That's for you, not me."

"Will you do it?"

"If I say no?"

"You run alone."

"I'll think about it."

"Do that," Coach said. He nodded, turned abruptly for his office, and left Mark alone on the field.

Mark, watching him go, waited until he was inside, muttered a soft, "Damn," and opened the door to the locker room. No comforting darkness met him. Every glaring light in the ceiling shone down on the chaos as ballplayers and runners tossed pads and sweats to the floor, hurled insults, and strutted in their gleaming bodies to the showers. Mark shouldered through the mob and found Dickie waiting beside his locker.

"Coach gives me a pain," he said.

"So what's new?"

Mark pulled his sweatshirt over his head and slammed it into his locker.

Dickie laughed.

Mark grinned. "You buy the beer."

3

A Blade of Cruelty

Moonlight spread like a white fan across the rippled creek that surged, dark and cold, cutting a deep pool under the willows hanging over the bank. Peanut, her hand circling dangerously low on Mark's stomach, giggled and nuzzled his ear. "It's okay," she said. He caught her hand, pushed it aside, sat up, and looked over his shoulder at his car. Dickie and Annette weren't in sight.

"Hey," Peanut cooed.

Mark turned. She had set her mouth in a mocking pout and rolled onto her back to tease him. Embarrassed and angry, he offered no response.

She shrugged and closed her blouse.

Mark watched her fingers climb up the buttons

towards her throat. He ached to start them down again. But he had fumbled, and she had laughed.

"Peanut?" he said.

Her fingers paused, allowing the blouse to fall open, but he had no will. He looked away. Her fingers moved, and when they reached her throat, she said, "Get me a beer." Obeying, he went to the car and banged on the roof. Dickie's head appeared before he could reach through the window.

"Peanut wants a beer."

"So get one from the trunk."

"I need the keys."

Dickie stretched over the back of the front seat, pulled them from the ignition and handed them through the window. "No more interruptions, okay?" Annette snickered, and Mark stood, miserably erect, afraid to see, as a slender white arm wrapped around Dickie's neck and pulled him to the seat.

Back beside the creek, Mark handed Peanut her beer and sat so his back was to her. Drinking, he watched the water. Willow leaves, like a school of minnows, drifted in the cold moonlight on the surface. The ground was hard and he shifted. A faint pain gripped his groin, eased, and spread like a chill up his spine. He finished his beer, the last swallow going down hard and tasteless, and flipped the bottle into the creek. It floated on its side, slowly half-filled, and bobbed, neck up. The current brought it back to his feet where it lodged in the tree roots.

Peanut draped herself over his back, reached her arms around his neck, and caressed his chest. "Some things know," she said.

"Know what?" Mark asked.

"How to stay up," she answered, gesturing to the bottle.

Tight in her arms, Mark felt small and weak. But he also felt anger harden him, and he turned to push her onto the ground. As they teetered off balance, he saw over her shoulder, Dickie and Annette coming from the car. He caught his falling weight, propped himself on his arm, and called, "Bring the beer."

Peanut loosed her arms from his neck, allowing one hand to drop to his lap. Quickly she touched him, whispered in his ear, and sat up straight. He collapsed, took a beer from Dickie, and stared morosely at the bottle in the water.

It was 2:30 A.M. before Mark dropped off Dickie and Annette and left Peanut at her house, but he didn't go straight home. He drove out a back road, rolled down the window, and cranked up the radio. The tuneless passion of Bobby Ridel's "Kissin Time" filled the car, and he pushed the accelerator to the floor. His headlights, like long fingers reached out and stroked the sides of the hills as the car wound through the valley. Wind wrapped coolly about his cheeks, and he leaned over the wheel into the throbbing music to beat the rhythm on the dash. The car became his world. But slowly the insistent pain he could not drive away rose in his groin. He pushed back against the seat adjusting his position. Finding no relief, he braked, made a U-turn, and headed home.

When he pulled into his drive, light shone from the kitchen window, and when he went inside, he found his father bundled in an old maroon robe sitting in the breakfast nook. "I've got to leak," Mark said, and rushed through the room. His father neither moved nor spoke.

In the bathroom Mark considered going to his room without returning to the kitchen, but he was hungry, and the pain, which hadn't been relieved, made him reckless. He went back.

His father spoke in a voice so muffled and distant Mark could hardly hear it, but he had heard what it was saying before. He opened the refrigerator and answered without questioning, "Sorry."

"Sorry comes cheap."

Mark set a quart bottle of milk on the counter and bent to see the lower shelves.

"I'm talking to you," his father said.

Mark glanced over his shoulder, continued rummaging, and muttered, "I'm not deaf."

His father raised his voice, "Where were you?"

Mark sighed and slowly placed a small, white paper-wrapped package of lunchmeat beside the milk. He opened the breadbox, took two slices of white bread from a loaf, and spread them with mustard. His father rose and crossed the room. Mark felt him coming but did not look up. "I went for a drive," he said.

His father grabbed him by the shoulder and spun him around. "What do you mean, you went for a drive? It's 3:30 A.M. No one goes for a drive at 3:30 A.M."

Mark turned back to his sandwich. "I did."

"Mark." His father's voice fell, its edge of anger dulled by weariness. "Who were you with?"

Mark heard the change and smiled. His pain tightened, grew sharp, and rose through him like a blade of cruelty. He closed the sandwich, took a large bite, picked up the milk, and faced his father. He met his gaze and held it, but he did not speak. He chewed and watched fear well like tears in the eyes before him.

"I was with Peanut," he said coldly.

His father stepped backward. "Mark," he started. "Your mother and I, you know we . . . mother and I . . . we don't approve of Peanut. She's . . . well, she's . . ." He halted, unable to say the word that would fix Mark's behavior in his mind.

"I know," Mark said. "She's fast."

His father drew a deep, sudden breath, seemed for an instant to grow large with anger, and then fall back into himself, broken.

Mark grinned at him, picked up his milk and crossed towards the table. As he went, he spoke. "Peanut and I, we, you know, get along." A piece of meat fell from his sandwich and landed at his father's feet. Stunned, his father stooped, picked it up, and crept from the room.

When he was gone, Mark sat, stretched his legs across the bench seat of the booth, and possessed the vacancy his father had left. He bit into his sandwich, his triumph feeding his hunger, but when he finished and lay quietly in the darkness of his room, the taste in his mouth was sour, and when he slept, he dreamed he was a small boy waking in the night because he had to pee. He got out of bed and, feeling along the wall, made his way to the door, but when he reached the place it should have been, he felt only wall. He groped beyond where he knew it was until he reached the corner and then returned. Again his fingers found only wall. He called, "Mommy." When he received no answer, he pounded on the wall and cried, "Where's my door?" Panicked, he found the windows a second time, and speaking out loud to control his fear reasoned, "The windows are to the left of the door." He followed the wall to the right until he bumped into the corner. He woke to his own scream, rolled from the bed, stumbled to the light, and switched it on. Stunned by the sudden brightness, he closed his eyes, but he leaned gratefully, his hand grasping the knob, against the door.

4

Psyched

It rained Saturday, a hard, driving rain through the morning. By afternoon the worst had passed, but the air hung thick with a cold mist, and puddles spread over low spots in the parking lot and along the course at Frick Park where the Owls ran their home meets. When the bus had pulled into the parking lot and stopped, Mark had claimed the back seat and stretched across it, ignoring the rapid, staccato chatter around him. Though he held himself still, he was anxious to move, and the wait rubbed at his nerves like an ill-fitting shoe. He closed his eyes and forced his tense hands to open and lie limp at his sides. But the effort to relax cost too much to sustain. He sat up and wiped the condensation from the window. Spectators stood clustered under umbrellas at the starting line. Others formed a ragged row across the field, a gauntlet of encouragement that would cheer the runners out and then, at the finish, urge them home. Still others, a group of laughing girls in plaid skirts and saddle shoes, sloshed across the parking lot and passed directly beneath his window. In the midst of this group, Mark saw Mary. He tapped on the glass. When she stopped and turned her face up to his, he scrawled "IH" on the window and grinned. She mouthed a reply he could not hear, but he read amusement in her eyes, so he stood, let the top half of the window down, and leaned out. "You're getting wet," he said.

"Think I'll shrink?" she asked.

"I hope not. You're small enough."

"Petite," she said. "Is it harder to run in the rain?"

"I'm a mudder."

"A mudder?"

"Yeah. A mean mudder. Nothing slows me down."

"Oh, if that's true, maybe you shouldn't come to the party tonight."

His stomach tightened. "I'm only fast at the races."

She smiled, "Then I'll see you there," tossed her head, and walked away. A vague uneasiness held him as he watched her go, and he was glad when Coach Gale called the team to the front for instructions.

"Central is a strong team," he said, "possibly the strongest we'll run against this year. To beat them you have to run smart."

He paused and looked directly at Mark. "First place isn't important. Applewhite is their best man. He's going to finish first or second no matter what. Their second and third men will score points. The key today is to run as a group and displace their fourth and fifth men. Mark, I want you to go out a little slower than usual. But only a little. I want a crisp pace, and I want everybody on it for the first mile and a half. After that, encourage each other, but push hard and do the best you can. If you can catch Applewhite, fine, but the team comes first."

Mark leaned forward, crossed his arms on the seat in front of him, and rested his chin on them. Without moving his head, he raised his eyes to watch his teammates scramble from the bus. Coach Gale stood in the aisle touching the runners and encouraging them as they filed past him. When the last one had stepped from the bus, Mark slowly pulled himself upright and stepped towards the exit. Coach stopped him, gripped his shoulder, and stared hard into his eyes. Staring back, Mark expected him to speak. Instead, he slowly tightened his fingers. Mark felt the pressure grow in his shoulder, and he tensed, holding his breath, as if his chest were being squeezed. He felt giddy. Then suddenly Coach loosened his grip. Mark exhaled, and with the release of his breath a silly smile vanquished the fixed emptiness of his face.

"You can do it," Coach said.

Mark jumped from the bus and walked quickly towards his teammates, but as he walked, he wondered what it was Coach said he could do. Not watching the ground, he splashed into an ankle-deep puddle, soaking his feet and legs. The cold brought him to attention, and he focused on the race.

"Baggs!" he yelled.

Baggs, who was halfway out of his sweatpants, looked up, tripped, hopped sideways to catch himself, and trampled the flapping pantleg in a puddle. "Here," he called. Mark jogged, his hands hanging loose at his sides, towards him.

Removing his dripping sweats, he asked, "Ready for this one?"

"I'm scared."

"You better be," Mark laughed. "It's part of being ready."

Baggs gaped. "You mean you're scared too!"

"Shitless," Mark grinned.

Baggs' face went blank, and then, as he searched for a reply, contorted into an uncomfortable smile. "I didn't think you would be," he said lamely.

Wishing he'd used a word more suitable to Baggs' scruples, Mark muttered, "Always." He leaned away and spit in the grass to give Baggs a chance to recover from his embarrassment. "Listen," he said when he straightened. "Stay with me today. Okay?"

"I'll try."

"Don't try. Stay with me."

Together they joined their teammates at the starting line where they were greeting the Central runners. Mark picked out Applewhite and shook his hand. "Feeling good?" he asked.

"Ready to run. You?"

"A little tight," Mark answered. "But it doesn't matter. Baggs here will push me."

Baggs stuck out his hand and laughed nervously, "Albert," he said.

Applewhite took it absently. "Luck," he said, but he looked questioningly at Mark, who smirked and said nothing.

When they were lined up to start, Mark nudged Baggs and motioned towards Applewhite who was staring towards them. "Wave," he said. Baggs glanced back and forth between Mark and Applewhite, seemed to question Mark, and then waved. Applewhite looked away quickly. "We've got him worried," Mark said. "He'll start too fast."

5
Gut It Out

At the gun, Applewhite burst to the front, as if he were running a sprint, and opened a ten-yard lead before the runners left the gauntlet. Mark made no attempt to stay with him. He went out slow, took Baggs and Simpson with him, and settled in behind Central's number-two man. Immediately behind them, the rest of the Owls bunched with Central's runners.

The Frick Park course was designed for large races. The first half mile was a wide open stretch run between the edge of a wood and a half dozen softball fields. At the end of it, the runners plunged down a short, steep hill to the lowest point on the course, crossed a wooden footbridge over a small stream, and then wound through a shaded picnic area to Killer Hill, a long gradual climb to the mile-and-a-half marker at the highest point on the course. Having conquered Killer Hill, runners often thought the last mile would be easy, but it wasn't. It was a punishing tear downhill, a sharp, almost 180-degree turn, and a flat, endless grind that retraced the first half mile to the finish.

Applewhite reached Killer Hill with a fifty-yard lead on the pack. From his position behind Central's second runner, Mark watched him and urged him on. *Run hard,* he thought. *Run your guts out and die on the stretch.* He glanced to his side. Baggs and Simpson were with him. "Ready?" he breathed. Neither spoke. In unison they moved with Mark and picked up the pace. The Central runner felt the change, leaned forward into the hill, and tried to hold his spot, but they drew beside him. For ten yards, twenty yards, they ran four abreast, and then the three pulled ahead. Silent, except for their breathing, they pushed up the hill. And as they did the sky darkened.

Slowly they gained on Applewhite. But Mark knew he wasn't coming back to them, and he was afraid of pressing too hard, for as he ran he understood what he had to do; he had to save Baggs and Simpson for the finish. When they reached the top of the hill, Applewhite led by thirty yards. They rolled over the crest and gave themselves to the pull of gravity. Quickly Mark's longer stride began to open a gap on Simpson and Baggs. "Stay with me," he said.

"Go," they urged.

Mark held back a moment pulling the others along, but he could feel them tiring. He glanced over his shoulder at Baggs and Simpson. "Don't quit," he said.

"Go," they repeated.

Mark looked ahead at Applewhite, gauged his pace,

and dropping his eyes to the path in front of him, yielded to the temptation of the downhill. He ran recklessly, foolishly stretching his stride over the rough ground, pitching himself forward to stay above his feet as he plunged ahead. The jarring impact of each stride shot through his legs and exploded in his stomach. His side, cramped by a stitch, ached, and he jammed a fist against it, but he had to let loose to keep his balance. Halfway down the hill he raised his eyes to Applewhite. A sour taste burned his throat, and his body tightened, for though he had closed the distance between them to ten yards, his wild descent had broken his rhythm, and Applewhite was running easily. Beyond him he could see a small cluster of figures at the sharp corner before the finishing straightaway. They were gesturing frantically, and as he neared, their cries rose above the rasp of his breath and the relentless pounding of his heart and feet in his ears.

"You can do it."

"Go get him, he's tired."

A crash of thunder drowned them. *They're wrong*, Mark thought. *I can't do it*. A cold shock of wind-driven rain hit him like a birdshot, and he slowed for the corner. Then a clear voice, Mary's, rose like a birdsong over the crackling crowd, "Come on, Mark!" He twisted slightly to find its source, and as he did, he felt his foot slide sideways in the mud.

As he slid his mind raced, *No one will blame me*. Deliberately, he pushed hard with the sliding foot. It went out from under him, and he crashed to his side, rolled once and slid, the icy mud caking his legs, arms, and face, to a stop in the crowd. He lay still in the mud, his pain frozen in the sudden silence following the screams of the crowd. A hand, its warmth searing like a cautery, touched him, and he sobbed.

Slowly, almost somnolently, knowing only regret that he could not stay face down in the mud, he pushed himself to his knees, stood, and forced his legs to move. Cheers began to penetrate his daze, and he stumbled forward. Still together, Baggs and Simpson came up to him. They parted to run to his left and right.

"Come on, Mark."

"Gut it out."

Awkwardly, his right arm hanging loose and bleeding at his side, his legs mudcaked, cold and stiffening, he lumbered between them.

"Come on, Mark," Baggs said.

"Come on, Mark," Simpson echoed.

Their words surrounded him. He ran contained in their chant as he ran contained in the rain that streamed with his tears down his face. And then they entered the gauntlet of cheering spectators. Faces, distorted by his blurring vision, loomed before him and disappeared. Voices called his name, Baggs' name, Simpson's name. They rose and fell as he was pulled forward by an urgency no longer his.

"Come on, Mark."

The burning at the back of his throat raged. He gasped, "I can't."

"You can," Baggs urged, and he took Mark's hand.

Light filled Mark's head, and he ran blind, reaching out his other hand to Simpson, who took it, and held it so that they ran as one body towards the finish. As they crossed it, Baggs and Simpson raised their arms, lifting Mark's in a sign of triumph. Then they released his hands, and he fell forward into the arms of Coach Gale.

6

Confession

Mark didn't want to arrive at the party alone, but Mary was social chairman of the Third Presbyterian Church youth group and had to be at the church early to decorate. He hadn't been invited to help, so he had no choice but to agree to meet her there. Feeling more anxiety than he realized, he had dressed carefully: pink shirt, black denims, and spit-polished spades. But when he walked in and looked over the crowded, brightly lit party room, he knew he had miscalculated. Every other male in the room was wearing a plaid sport shirt, cotton chinos, and white bucks. Without others dressed as he was, there was no one to admire his pose. Nor did it help that Mary only waved to him from beyond the sofas and chairs arranged in a circle for conversation and continued setting out cookies and punch on a long white table. He started towards her, feeling as if he had gotten a wrong message and had appeared in a costume, but she disappeared into the kitchen, and Baggs called to him across the room.

"Mark. Over here." Helplessly he turned aside and wound his way through small clusters of chattering girls to Baggs who stood in the center of a group of joking guys at the edge of the conversation area. Before Mark could greet him, Baggs enthused, "Great race, Mark. I'd of never had the guts to finish like you did."

"Sure you would."

"Listen to him will ya?" Baggs continued. "He hits that mud at the turn, falls smack on his face. Look at how he's all scraped up, and his legs are worse. He gets up, grinds it out to the finish before collapsing, and then says anybody could do it."

Mark touched his face. Underneath the brush burn across his cheek, he felt himself flush, and he wished the lights were lower. "It doesn't do much for my good looks, does it?" he said. Then, realizing a number of girls had joined the group, he laughed self-consciously.

A short stocky fellow Mark had never met quipped, "It's not so bad. I thought it was a reflection from your shirt."

A ripple of nervous laughter started across the group and died when Mark stiffened and stepped towards the joker, who stood his ground, stuck out a hand, and said, "Jim Gaines, I've heard a lot about you."

"Then you have the advantage," Mark said, taking the hand and squeezing.

"Yeah. I guess I do," Jim answered, looking Mark in the eye. He smiled and slowly tightened his grip. "I'm Mary's cousin. She told me to be sure and meet you."

"Well, you have," Mark said. "I'm sure the pleasure's all yours."

"It is." Jim laughed openly and released Mark's hand. "I'm glad you've come."

Baggs, seeing the moment of tension had passed, pushed between them. "You should have seen the finish, Jim. It was great. Applewhite won, but the three of us, Mark, Simpson and me, we came across together, just like Coach Gale wanted, so we won the meet."

Mark slipped aside and drifted towards the food, arriving at the table just as Mary returned with a basket of potato chips. He reached for one, but she dipped the basket low evading his hand, and said, "Not yet. No food till the blessing."

"When's that?"

"When Coach Gale gets here."

"Coach Gale? Here?"

"Yes."

"What for?"

"He's our speaker tonight."

"You have speakers at parties?"

"Well, not exactly. We have a devotional time at the end. Coach Gale often gives it. He's an elder and runs the church's summer camp, so he keeps pretty close to us during the year."

Mark snitched a potato chip, popped it in his mouth, and grinned. "You set me up."

"Are you mad?"

"Is the door locked?"

"No."

"Then I'm not mad." When Mary looked up at him, puzzled, Mark laughed. "As long as the door's open, I'm free to leave."

"It wasn't really fair of me, was it?"

"Was Coach in on it?"

"No. And I didn't really plan it. I wasn't sure I wanted to go out with you when you asked me, but I didn't want to say no, and this party just popped into my mind."

Mark paused, started to answer, then changed his mind. "Tell me about Jim," he said.

"He's my cousin."

"I know that. I also know he has a grip like a mill hand."

"He's a wrestler."

"You could have warned me. Why don't I know him?"

"He goes to a prep school in New York. He's only around on vacations."

"Well, he's not shy. Why didn't you want to go out with me?"

Startled by the sudden shift backwards in the conversation, Mary stepped away from Mark and did not speak.

"My friends?" he asked.

"I don't want to talk about people," she answered. "Besides, I didn't say I wouldn't. I said I wasn't sure."

"When will you be?"

"What?"

"Sure."

"It seems we're back where we started," she said. "Let's join the others." She took his arm and steered him towards a group talking to a tall young man in a madras sport coat. "I want you to meet our youth leader."

The youth leader had obviously been primed, for as they drew nearer, he turned to them. "You must be

Mark. I'm Henry. Mary told me you were coming. Welcome to Third Pres."

Awkward, unsure of what to answer, Mark muttered, "Yeah, glad to be here, I guess."

Mary laughed and covered for him. "The food's ready, Henry. Don't you think we should get this party going?"

"Good idea." Henry stepped aside from the group and called out, "Okay, everybody, gather around." Mary squeezed Mark's arm, and whispered, "Relax."

"Easy for you," he answered.

Mary laughed. "Stick with me," she said taking his arm in her hands and grinning. They moved in with the others, and Henry prayed.

Then they played games. By the time Coach Gale arrived, late in the evening, Mark had held a lifesaver on a toothpick in his mouth and transferred it to the toothpick Mary held in hers without stabbing her lips. He'd grasped an orange under his chin and without appearing too fresh or dropping it twisted sideways so Mary could take it under hers. And he'd easily found his shoes in the jumbled pile of white bucks in the sock race. The only thing about the evening that surprised him was that he enjoyed himself. In Mary's presence he forgot his need to stand aloof, and he found an easiness that allowed him to laugh without mocking.

When Coach Gale came in, Mark went directly to him. "I didn't expect to see you," he joked. "Do you think I can take another pep talk?"

To Mark's chagrin, Coach Gale ignored his tone. "Was the first one hard?"

"Harder than I expected."

Coach Gale reached out his hand, rested it on Mark's

shoulder, just as he had in the bus, looked into his face, and sighed. After a long silence, he said, "I'm sorry. I expect it was harder than I ever intended." He shook his head sadly and turned to join Henry.

Puzzled, Mark watched him cross the room. For an instant his focus held Coach firm, and then suddenly Coach slipped away. Applewhite was ahead of him turning the corner, and he was plunging after him. A clear voice rose from across the room, and he was once again sliding towards his irrevocable fall.

"No," he said out loud, and then Mary was at his side.

"You have to," she said.

"Have to what?"

"Come sit down. They're going to start."

"Oh," he said. "I was just remembering this afternoon."

Mary looked up at him. Quietly, she said, "It bothers you a lot, doesn't it?"

He nodded.

"Don't let it. You didn't try to fall."

Startled, Mark stared blankly at Mary. He felt tired. The afternoon rain beat on his face. His spirit broke, and he felt himself pitch into his fall. "No," he said. "No."

"Then come on," Mary said. "Let's get the sofa."

Mark slouched against the arm of the sofa and dropped his hand onto Mary's beside him. When she did not move it, he settled into the cushion and looked up smiling, amused at the circumstances that had led him into a prayer meeting, curious to hear what Coach Gale, who stood silently, completely at ease, surveying the group, would say.

"I came here prepared to talk about resisting temptation," Coach Gale began. "But, now that I'm here, now that I'm looking into your faces, I sense the Spirit wants me to speak of something else.

"I'm afraid I may embarrass Mark and Albert, but I ask them to bear with me, for I think something remarkable happened this afternoon, and I want to reflect on it with you.

"You all know the story of the tortoise and the hare. The hare is an arrogant fellow, an egotistical bully who deserves to be taken down several notches. But he can run. At the start of the race he dashes off and opens such a great lead, he lies down to nap. The turtle, the faithful, slow turtle, a type of the good man, passes him as he sleeps, plugs on, crosses the finish line, and wins the race.

"It's a great story. As a coach, I love it, and whenever I hear the phrase, 'The race is not to the swift,' I think of the tortoise and the hare. But in Scripture, the source of the phrase, the phrase has a very different meaning. In Scripture the swift are grouped with the strong, the wise, and the understanding. They are the righteous, the ones who deserve to win. And Scripture tells us they lose.

"Ecclesiastes 9, verse 11. 'I returned, and saw under the sun, that the race is not to the swift, nor the battle to the strong, neither yet bread to the wise, nor yet riches to men of understanding, nor yet favor to men of skill; but time and chance happeneth to them all.'

"This afternoon most of you watched a race that Mark and Albert ran. Had the race been to the swift, Mark would have won it. But Mark didn't win, he fell, and a slower runner won. All of this you know. You saw it. I want to tell you what you probably don't know."

Mark stirred uneasily on the sofa. Coach turned to him. "I shouldn't single you out this way, I know, but I want you to understand, and I want everyone else to understand what you did today."

"But Coach, you can't know," Mark blurted.

Coach Gale raised his hand, gesturing, and Mark, his head dropping to his chest, fell silent. "Mark's right," he said. "At the deepest level I don't know, not what he knows."

Mark snapped his head up.

"But this I do know. Before the race, I asked Mark to run, not for himself, but for the team. I asked him to pace Albert and the others for the first mile and a half. He did that for me, for the team, and because of it he lost. His action, though I'm sure he has not thought of it this way, was profoundly Christlike and should stand as a challenge to each of us.

"But there is more. The last mile Mark went out on his own. And we saw what happened. Trying to catch Applewhite, he pushed too hard. At the limit of his ability, he fell. As we all do. Then Albert and Simpson picked him up. Those Mark had carried, carried him, and together they came home.

"And this is what I want to say: Look hard at those three running the race, for in their bearing each other forward we have an image of our dependence on each other. We have an image of the body of Christ alive in the world."

The drive from the church to Mary's was short. Mark made it, his hands closed on the wheel, his eyes straight ahead. He could sense Mary close beside him. Her silence invited him to speak, but he knew the words building in him, once uttered, would somehow change him forever, and he was not ready to hear them.

When they reached her house, he shut off the

engine, jumped out, and said quickly, "I'll walk you to the door." But Mary did not move. The roof light shone on her face, and in her openness he saw a possibility he had never before imagined.

"Not yet," she said.

He got back in the car and pulled the door shut. The light went out, and in the darkness he felt something in himself loosen.

"You want to talk," Mary said.

"That's not a question, is it?" Mark asked.

"Call it an offer."

Mark sighed and leaned onto the steering wheel. "I don't get it," he said.

"What's there to get?"

"You. Coach."

Mary said nothing, by silence forcing Mark to go on.

"You scare me."

"I don't mean to."

"But you want something I've never had to give, something I'm not even sure I have to give."

"Everyone has it."

"Do they?" Mark turned towards her and challenged, "Tell me what it is."

"The truth," Mary said simply.

Mark laughed a short, gasping burst of a laugh and twisted around to look out the window. When he spoke his voice had hardened to an edge that scratched down the glass like a fingernail. "The truth," he said. "I'll tell you the truth. All that stuff Coach said. He doesn't know shit. I'm no more Christlike than Judas himself. I fell on my face out there this afternoon because I quit. You hear me, I quit. Applewhite was ahead, and I couldn't catch him, and I couldn't take it, so I fell on my face and quit."

Mary touched his shoulder, "You got up."

"Sure. When it was too late to make any difference."

"It made a difference."

"I still lost."

"But didn't you hear Coach? Those you carried, carried you. That's the part that counts. That's the part he wanted you to hear. That's the part he wanted us all to hear."

Mark turned back to Mary. "That's the part I can't understand."

"You will," she answered. "Let's go in. I want you to meet my folks."

"Not tonight."

"You'll have to meet them sometime."

"Why's that?"

"I'm not allowed to go out with a guy they haven't met."

Mark got out of the car, walked around it, and opened Mary's door. "Let's go," he said.

Part Four
1960

1

Nightwatch

A day at the Third Presbyterian Girls' Camp ended with cabin devotions for the campers, but after lights out, the counselors—high-school and college girls—remained on duty for an hour before the nightwatch came on. No hour of the day seemed longer. And now that there had been a prowler, the wind winding through the treetops and dipping to the ground making dry, shuffling noises in the old leaves carpeting the woods, seemed dangerous. The soft whispers of the girls not ready for sleep buzzed behind the canvas flaps that had been rolled down, closing the half-walled cabins. The counselors, working in pairs, walked the paths, quieting the girls with their presence, speaking only when the whispers broke into laughter.

Mary stood alone at the door of the cabin furthest from the lights of the central bathhouse. Against the distant glow of the yellow bug light, she could see her partner on guard outside the first cabin in the row. She wished she had the central position. The scraping of a branch against another in the wind unsettled her, and she turned to peer into the woods, but she could see nothing.

A pillowed sob sounded near her. She went quickly to the cabin door and spoke.

"It's all right. I'm here."

A small voice answered, "I'm scared."

"You and me both," Mary said under her breath, before drawing aside the door flap, stepping into the cabin, and sitting on the floor beside the child's bed. "I'll stay with you," she said and gently began to rub her back.

"Will you stay all night?"

"If you want me to."

"I do."

"Then I will."

The child lay quiet under Mary's hand. Outside the wind moaned through the trees and scuffed along the ground. Mary fingered the switch on the flashlight in her lap, and shifted against the bed.

"You won't let him get me?" the child asked.

Mary stiffened, her hand stopped its circular movement on the child's back and then started again. "No. I won't let him get you." The wind lifted the canvas flaps, banging the weights against the walls. Catching her breath, Mary sang in a hoarse whisper, "God is watching over you, watching over you . . . ," and the child settled into sleep.

* * *

A small, cramped room off the staff quarters served as the camp office. Coach Gale had furnished it with an oversized wooden desk, two filing cabinets, three painted wicker chairs, and an elaborate P.A. system. Back issues of *The Runner,* cellophane wrapped packages of camp tee shirts, sweaters, and jackets were stacked neatly on shelves behind the desk. Coach Gale had the P.A. system switched to the room speakers, and the complex counterpoint of a Bach fugue played off the walls. When Mark came in, Coach turned it down and motioned Mark to a seat. "I've got something new for you," he said, and handed him a heavy, two-foot-long, sealed beam flashlight.

Mark hefted it and slapped it repeatedly into the palm of his left hand as if it were a nightstick. "You're worried?"

"I have to be."

"So you expect him back?"

"I'm hoping otherwise."

"Yeah." Mark rose, crossed the room, and stared out into the dark. "And if he shows?"

"That's what the light's for. Try to see his face. But don't get close, and try not to wake the campers."

"What if he comes for me?"

"He won't."

"You can't be sure."

"Trust me."

Mark looked at the clock. "The counselors will be starting down. Time to move."

* * *

Mark stood for a moment outside the office looking up at the sky. Directly over his head the Big Dipper poured out its nightly portion of joy. For the first few weeks of camp Mark had liked nightwatch. He liked the cool wind and the surprising noises. He had learned from many camping trips that the same creatures inhabit the woods at night as inhabit it by day, and he had learned to walk without a light. But now nightwatch was different. The closeness of the dark was alien, no longer familiar. Something, someone who was not there during the day was out there, and instead of standing in the easy dark, he stood, armed with nothing more than a light, between the sleeping girls and a waking nightmare.

Halfway up the hill Mark met the counselors coming down in a group to relax, eat, and talk in the lounge before returning to their cabins for the night. "All quiet?" he asked.

"Almost," one answered. "Mary's in with the girl who saw him."

"Okay. I'll see if she wants to come down in a little while." Mark left the counselors and entered the trimmed, parklike woods of the cabin area. Three double rows of cabins reached like wheel spokes from the lighted hub of the bathhouse to the rim of a circling path. Mark's first stop was the bathhouse. "Anybody here?" he called. When he received no answer, he entered. He opened each stall and looked into the shower. A luna moth clung to a bath towel left on a hook. Though it was not the first one he'd ever seen, he stepped nearer to it to get a better look. The four-inch wings were bright green, but soft like cotton, and smooth like mint ice cream. He reached for it, then, realizing touching it would destroy the wings, he withdrew his hand and carefully lifted the towel from the hook, carried it outside, and draped it over a pine bough beyond the circle of light.

Except for the occasional creak of a cot as a camper shifted in her sleep and the rise and fall of the wooing wind, the camp was quiet. Mark moved down the spoke opposite Mary's. When he reached the path marking the perimeter of the area, he turned and started around the loop. At the end of the second spoke, he left the path and worked away from the cabins through the untrimmed woods. He came out of them and stood at the edge of a meadow. Backing against an oak, making himself invisible against the black bark, he watched the headlights moving up and down the highway in the valley below. He looked hard, but the darkness was impenetrable. "Could use a little moonlight," he said to himself, and then he thought of Mary and how they'd walked and laughed in the meadow before these nights of fear. She'd be wanting to go down to the lounge. He ducked back under the trees, pushed aside the low branches, and crunched down the path so she'd hear him coming and not be surprised.

She was standing in front of the cabin as he approached.

"Don't wake the girls," she whispered.

"You want to go to the lounge?" he asked.

"No." He looked at her, questioning. "I told her I'd stay. Would you bring my sleeping bag to me? I'll sleep on the floor."

Mark looked over his shoulder through the woods. "This is the worst cabin to be in, you know. We figure the guy came in through the meadow and up this way."

"I know. That's why I'm staying."

"You're crazy."

"No. Scared."

"You know," he said, taking her hand and walking slowly towards the woods, "I meant it last night."

"I know," she said quietly.

"Then come with me. Tomorrow's your day off. My uncle's cabin's miles from here. No one will ever know."

"That's not my concern."

Mark turned to her, catching her other hand. "What is your concern?"

"I want a future."

He dropped her hands. "You're saving yourself," he said bitterly.

"Not just myself," she answered.

"So there's no chance."

"None."

"I better get your sleeping bag."

He started down the spoke towards the counselors' cabin. "Mark?" Her voice stopped him. When he looked back, she stepped near to him and said, "You know it's right this way?"

He shrugged.

"Tell me, I need to know you know."

"It's right," he said, the morose tone of his voice breaking the tension, making them both laugh.

She kissed her fingers, touched them to his lips, and slipped away into the cabin.

* * *

After the counselors returned to their cabins, Mark made a slow loop around the area, finishing at 12:30. He went down the hill, circled the staff building, checked the lock on the craft hall, and entered the kitchen. He found the lunch the cooks had made up for him and filled a thermos with the last of the day's coffee. It was thick and bitter like a slice of darkness. "Drink a cup of this stuff," he said out loud, "you can drink anything." He tucked the thermos and lunch in a knapsack and went back up the hill. Finding the cabin area quiet, he crossed the perimeter path and moved through the trees to the base of the oak he had rested against earlier. He sat, poured himself coffee, and searched the dark meadow for movement.

An hour passed. An occasional car sped down the road. He watched for one to slow, stop, and turn off its lights. But none did. He ate his sandwich and drank more coffee. He stood up, stretched, and walked a short ways into the field. Suddenly he tensed.

Fifty yards away a hunched figure darted from a depression Mark had been unable to see into and disappeared. Mark dropped to his hands and knees, wondering if he'd been seen. He scuttled, bent over, back to his tree, grabbed his light, and slipped into the cover of the woods. Slowly, with great care, he worked quietly to intercept the figure. Coming near the edge of the trees, Mark saw the figure in the meadow. As dark as the night was, the heavy shape stood dark against the sky. But it was no longer moving towards him.

Mark waited. A low, almost tuneless, humming reached him. The figure bent, working at something on the ground. Mark stepped forward.

"What are you doing?" he demanded, shining his light full in the figure's face. The figure jumped backward, dropping a pack, and growled unintelligibly. Mark followed the face with his light, and he realized he had been imagining a different face, a younger one, perverse and sensual, but harmless. The face before him was vagrant, evil, capable of more than glaring from the dark. Threatened, he stepped back and stared. Thick black eyebrows met over the bridge of the nose, hiding small furtive eyes. Beneath them, the mouth twisted sharply to one side as if pulled by mocking fingers.

"Get the light out," it snarled.

Mark dropped the light to the man's chest and spoke. "This is private property," he said. "You have to move on."

The man motioned to his pack.

"You can't stay here," Mark said. "This is a private camp."

The man, seeming to pay no attention, stooped to his pack and started to untie the knotted drawstring.

"You can't stay here," Mark repeated. When the man ignored him, he said, "Look, you'll have to come with me to see the camp director. Maybe he'll give you a bed."

Without straightening, the man turned towards Mark. The short, silver barrel of a small bore pistol glistened in the beam of Mark's light.

"I ain't going nowhere," he said. "Now shut that light out and throw it over here."

Mark did as he was told.

Instantly the man was on it. He laughed a low, guttural laugh, choked it off, and said, "Now I see." A sharp stab of light blinded Mark.

"No," he begged. "Please. Don't."

Then the light went out, and the pounding of feet fleeing towards the highway filled his ears like music. For a long moment he stood motionless, then he turned and walked back into the trees. Branches he could not see cut his face, but far off, flickering, he could see the light at the center of the camp.

2

The Cabin

During the long climb up the mountain, Mark grew tense. The needle on the temperature gauge of his old Chevy crawled steadily towards the H. It was wavering at the edge of danger when he downshifted and turned off the pavement onto the dirt road that led downhill to the cabin. The engine roared, slowed, and settled into a steady drone holding the car back on the steep grade. The car pitched from pothole to pothole. The needle fell back towards normal, and Mark relaxed.

The sun cut through the quivering aspens and cast a netlike pattern of quick motion on the yellow road. Now and again a short bright dart lay caught in it—a red eft basking in the early summer warm. Mark steered around them. Memories of the hundreds of newts he had caught, confined in coffee cans, and taken home with him as a boy washed over him, and he laughed remembering the day he had spilled a can of them in the car. One had crawled from the accelerator onto his mother's sandaled foot just as they rounded a bend to come face to face with a black bear. His mother had looked from the bear, which stood on its hind legs and stared into the windshield, to the newt on her foot. No doubts weakened her resolve. She screamed, flung open the door, and charged the bear.

The grade leveled, and the road curved around the side of the mountain. Mark watched the sun disappear in the rearview mirror, shifted into high, and let the car idle along. A quiet, as chilling as the shade settled on him, and he shivered. When the road turned sharply downhill again and began to follow a stream, he hunched his shoulders, sat forward, and began to watch the water. It was low, barely a trickle between the pools. But in the pools, deep clear crescents cut around and under granite boulders, which the sun never reached, native brook trout thrived. Mark had taken his first fish from one the summer his father and uncle had built the cabin, and he loved the stream as he loved no other.

Driving along, he could feel in his hands the sharp cold of the water, and he knew the fish would be there. He stopped the car, got out, and walked ahead to where the stream curved away from the road. He slipped down the bank and cut across the bend of the stream through the trees. Ahead of him a dying beech, its roots undercut, leaned over a long narrow pool. Stepping lightly, he approached it, braced a hand on its trunk, and bent over the stream. A quick shadow shot into the darkness beneath the roots. Mark smiled, turned, and went back through the trees.

* * *

When he reached the cabin, he pulled the car onto the grass and parked, but he did not get out. He sat. The afternoon sun streaming into the clearing splashed across the white block side of the cabin, flowed onto the lawn, and spread into a shallow pool of wavering green. Mark squinted and covered his eyes. He imagined the day the way he had dreamed it: the cabin, the sun, and Mary beside him. For a moment he drifted in reverie. Then the light died as a cloud passed over the clearing, and Mark, feeling the shadow, opened his eyes. He turned to the empty seat beside him.

From the far side of the lawn the low burble of the spring reached him. He crawled from the car, crossed the grass, knelt at the low stone wall arced against the mountainside, and dipped his hands into the water held behind it. He drank. Then, scooping the water from the overflow, he rinsed his face and slicked back his hair. "Am I dumb," he said out loud, and shook his head.

He went through the cabin, raising all the windows and propping open the bedroom doors to allow the wind to blow the mustiness out. He went back to the spring, dipped a bucket of water, returned, filled the tea kettle, and put it on the propane stove to heat. Then he swept the floor, rolled out his sleeping bag, stocked the cabinet over the kitchen sink with the bread, soup, canned spaghetti, and cereal he had brought, and laid a fire in the fireplace. The kettle whistled as he finished. "Perfect," he said. He spooned instant coffee and sugar into a mug, poured the boiling water into it, and went out onto the sunlit porch.

He propped his foot on the rail, leaned forward on

his knee, and sipped. Full shade blanketed the clearing, and the breeze, edged with coolness, promised good sleeping. He laced his fingers around the mug, cupping its warmth in his palms, and breathed in the coffee smell. From the blackness a blank, distorted face peered back at him. He stared at it for several moments and then tipped it slightly. The face disappeared. He tipped it back. The face slid into view. He lifted it to his lips and drank. Instantly, he jerked upright. The boiling coffee sloshed over his hand and spilled across his crotch. He flung the cup into the air and danced howling across the porch, pulling his jeans away from his skin.

But the splash across his pants cooled quickly. He laughed, "So much for lust, hotshot," and settled into a wooden lawn chair, stretched his feet out, and mused.

He thought of Mary, of the months he'd been dating her, of the hours he'd spent in church almost believing because he knew how she wanted him to. And he thought of himself, of his stupid blundering towards intimacy, of the impossibility of his invitation. He wanted to feel rejected, but he felt somehow purged as if his asking had put before him his own confused feelings. And as the falling sun washed him in light, he was glad Mary had not come, for in the quiet of his solitude he understood had she said yes she would have betrayed herself, and the Mary he wanted would have left him forever.

The narrow wood slats of the chair grew hard. The sun fell below the trees, and the air cooled. Mark stirred, shifting to get comfortable. Then he rose and yawned. "Might as well fish," he said.

3

Brook Trout

Mark worked upstream. Using small red worms for bait, he caught and killed two brookies about eight inches long. When he sighted the overhanging beech, he leaned his rod against a tree and climbed onto a large boulder to see. Though the pool was no more than fifteen feet long, fishing it was going to be tough. A wedge of granite shaping a rough dam and spillway formed the foot of the pool. The far bank where the current worked under the tree dropped sharply to the water, forming the belly of a crescent. It curved away from Mark and then returned to fall into a crumbling pile of stones over which the stream trickled as it entered the pool. Nearest him the bank was grown up in thumb-thick beech.

Mark slipped off the rock, picked up his rod, and walked up the stream bed. Twenty feet from the wedge he stopped and knelt. He nipped the number 8 hook and the BB split shot from his line, dug in his vest pocket for his container of hooks, and removed the smallest he had, a number 16. Squinting, he tied it to his line, then buried it in a worm. Satisfied no hook showed, he half rose and crept nearer the pool. A small branch, fallen from the beech, floated across the surface.

One cast, he thought. *I either catch him or spook him.*

Mark released the bail on the reel, and caught the line with his finger. Slowly he raised the rod, tracing an arc that stopped behind his head. He ducked lower to clear the branches sweeping low from the trees, sighted his target, an imaginary circle just short of the drifting twigs, and cast.

The worm, too light to pull the line forward, seemed to float in the air. It found a slip of wind, halted, and fell sideways, curving back under the line. It hit the ground halfway up the bank beneath the beech and lodged against a root. The line fell across the water, bowing slightly in the weak current, and sank. Mark tensed and held his breath. The culprit wind ran through his hair and down his cheek like a lotion-softened hand. Untouched he waited. The water wavered before him and blurred. Jagged lines of light, graphing his patience, distorted his vision. He blinked and breathed out. The stream returned.

Cautiously, to avoid snagging, he began to reel. The worm dragged over the root, tumbled towards the stream, and disappeared into the dark water undermining the tree. The line went limp. Mark caught it in his left hand, let it run loosely over his forefinger, and waited. At the same moment he felt the pull, the line straightened, inscribing a slashing diagonal from his bent rod tip to the water. He hauled back and stood. The diagonal veered up the pool. Mark eased the tension, letting the fish run. When the line snagged the floating leaves, he tightened the drag. The fish slowed and turned. But it was not tired. Using the current, it rushed the length of the pool, then swerved for the deep water under the bank. Mark gave line, stepped to the foot of the pool, and then snubbed the run. Feeling the hook, the fish twisted back and rose to the surface. Mark grinned, "Gotcha now." Though the brookie made three more runs, darting towards the cover under the beech, each time the dancing rod brought it back weakened. Mark raised the rod higher and higher, working him into the shallows. Exhausted, the brookie turned side up and floated motionlessly. Keeping enough line out to stop a last panicked run, Mark bent, slipped his hand under the fish and lifted him from the stream.

He worked the hook loose and then, grasping him by the jaw, held him up. "Must be nearly twelve inches," he said. The mottled side of the fish flashed iridescent blues, and the square tail curled as the fish hung from his grip. Mark laid it on a patch of moss and took his knife from its sheath. He balanced the blade in his fingers and poised to crack it on the head. But he stopped. "No," he said.

He pulled a short, nylon cord stringer from his vest and threaded it in through the fish's mouth and out its gills. Then, walking quickly, he carried the trout to the cabin spring. He removed the stringer and held the fish in the water. Slowly he moved it back and forth, working the water through the gills which began to open and shut rhythmically. He loosened his grip. The fish spread its fins. He let go, and the fish swam from his hand.

4

Face to Face

When he crawled into his sleeping bag, Mark did not sleep. He would close his eyes, and the fish would swim into his sight. He would raise his hand to kill it. Then it would be gone, and Mary would be walking away from him. He'd start to speak, to reach out to stop her, but he'd have no voice. He'd turn, shift his pillow, and groan. When at last he slept, he dreamed.

He was sitting under the tree overlooking the meadow. Halfway down it a hunched figure rose from a depression. Behind it the red glow of a fire appeared. Faint music drifted towards him. Other shadowy shapes, circling the fire, joined the first. Somehow he knew he knew them, so he rose and went forward. As he moved through the field, he felt himself grow small until he was a mere nub of fear. Then the hunched figure, an old man with a long gray beard, stepped from the circle. He took his hand, drew him from the world, and led him to a willowy and laughing girl. He joined their hands, stepped aside and took up a fiddle. The circle closed, and he began calling a square dance. Mark gave himself to it. Whirling with the girl on his arm, he became part of the pattern, a community in consort, united in joy. And then he saw the girl was Mary.

Suddenly the music ended. The dance dissolved. The dancers scattered. Mary held his hand and led him through the woods. Huge footsteps pounded behind them. Though they pushed through the grassblades and scrambled over sticks and stones, they were too slow. Mary fell, cowering. "Get up! Run!" Mark pleaded. He turned. Though he died, whatever followed would not harm her. A human hand reached down and lifted him into the air. He fought and wriggled as it drew him close to a pasty, empty face. Then he screamed. The face was his own.

He woke. The square of window above the bed was gray with morning mist. He lay still and focused on it until the terror of the dream passed. "Jesus," he whispered. He unzipped the sleeping bag, sat up, and dropped his feet to the floor. The cold shot through his soles. "Jesus," he said again. The room closed around him and the panic of the dream returned. He pulled on his pants, crossed the room, and went out onto the porch.

Though the dark was gone, no sunlight reached over the mountain into the clearing. He still had hours to sleep, but he wanted full wakefulness. Barefooted and shirtless, he waded into the mist. When he reached the spring, he knelt carelessly on the wet stones and scooped handful after handful of water onto his face. The cold shocked his skin. It ran down his chest and into his pants. He shivered, but he plunged his hands deeper into the spring to pull armfuls of water over his head. Gasping he cried, "Jesus," and hung, braced on the rocks, over the pool. The water stilled.

His face, hair ragged and wet, eyes staring wildly, appeared before him. "Bastard," he said. It seemed to laugh. Then through it he saw the trout holding behind the eyes. He leaned sideways to see, but as he moved the face stretched like a rubber mask. He rose on his arms. It shrank, but the water caught the sky and he saw nothing. He let himself back down. As if to embrace it, he bent nearer. And then slowly, giving himself to the face, he immersed his head. The water covered him. He opened his eyes to see, inches away, the trout hovering effortlessly. Face to face with the trophy he'd spared, Mark, at last, knew as he was known.

Nightwatch was typeset in Caledonia, a face designed by W. A. Dwiggins in 1938, based on an 18th-century Scottish model.

Nightwatch was set on a Mergenthaler Linotron 202/N; Judy Schafer, compositor. Printed by R. R. Donnelley of Harrisonburg, Virginia.